I0571929

The Rainy Season

J. Adams

The Rainy Season

J. Adams

J. Adams

Copyright © 2014, 2017 J. Adams
Jewel of the West Publishing
All Rights Reserved
ISBN-13: 978-0615992068
ISBN-10: 0615992064
Library of Congress Control Number: 2014905331

Jewel of the West™
P U B L I S H I N G

The Rainy Season

J. Adams

Life is a fickle thing, and destiny is as unpredictable as the shifting of the wind.

When I was ten years old, I wasn't concerned about either of those things until the day my mother died. That single event changed the course of my life, pointing me towards a destiny I could never have foreseen, and a love I couldn't have forsaken even if I tried.

J. Adams

Chapter 1

Seattle, Washington – March, 2006

Sitting on the side of the bed with my arms around my backpack, I waited for my new family to come and take me away.

The couple were old friends of my mother's and everything had been arranged; when Mama passed on from the cancer, I was to live with Gina and Marco de Francesco and become a part of their family–a plan I wasn't informed of until the reading of her will. I met the de Francescos the summer before when they came to visit. Daddy had just died in a car accident and they came to support Mama.

They had one son, Gilles. We shared the same birthday, July 25th. Like me, he was an only child. Gilles was very tall for his age. At only fifteen, he was well over six feet. He was a wrestler in school, so he was very muscular. Five years older than me, he had become my friend and my support that summer, talking and spending time with me during the day, and comforting me during the nights that I would awaken from bad dreams, nights when Mama was too emotionally exhausted to get up. Gilles would sit in the rocking chair in my room and hold me, quieting my fears, giving me new dreams to lull me back to sleep. And now he would be my brother.

Lost in thought, I looked around my bare room. I was about to move away from everything I had ever known. The house was sold and all my things were packed up and shipped. Some of Mama's things were shipped as well, little keepsakes for me. The rest were sold, the money put into a savings account for me.

I missed Mama so much. I missed Daddy too.

But while Daddy had been my sun and moon, Mama had been my whole world, my universe. My only other relative was an uncle who was a resident in the state mental hospital and would be there for the rest of his life. I remembered seeing him a few times when I was little. He played with me and made weird noises, jerking his head a lot. Tourette's Syndrome is what Mama said it was. She used to visit him on a regular basis. There was no one left to visit him now. I wondered if he would miss Mama, or if her absence would even matter.

"Come on, pretty girl, it's time to go." Gilles' voice was soft as he entered my room.

Standing, I slipped my arms through the straps of my backpack and grabbed my ballet bag, something I definitely could not leave behind. I had taken ballet since I was five and hoped to continue in Park City. I stood for another moment, looking around my room, feeling so lost. Gilles took my hand and we walked downstairs where Gina and Marco were waiting.

"Did you remember everything?" Gina asked. "Once we're on the road, there's no turning back."

I nodded at this woman who would be taking Mama's place in a way. She was the kind of woman Mama would call high maintenance–very fashionable with her perfectly-styled, chic haircut, red manicured nails, designer outfit, plucked brows, and year-round tan. Gina was the polar opposite of Mama. Mama was what you would call a minimalist. She used to wear only a hint of makeup on her dark skin, her hair was wash and wear, the tight curls uniform and reaching her shoulders. She liked sundresses and sandals in the summer, and denims and soft sweaters in the winter. Hers was a natural beauty that radiated warmth and reflected its own elegance. The two women were as different as night and day. There was nothing bottled or packaged about Mama. I couldn't say the same about her friend.

Gina's husband, Marco, owned a foreign sports car business and was always dressed casually–the opposite of his wife–and therefore much more approachable, even though he was built like a muscleman. Gilles was a younger version of his dad with his tousled, black hair and ocean-blue eyes.

I couldn't help wondering where I would fit in their world. Being the product of a Nigerian-born mother and a Welsh father, people always told Mama I was a beautiful child, that I was a friendly and helpful child. Angelic was what they called me. But would that be enough to fit in with this new life? I didn't know, but I truly hoped so.

Smiling, Marco took my free hand. "Let's go, *bella*."

We exited the house and Marco locked the door, placing the key in the lock box hanging on the knob. I got in the back seat with Gilles and peered through the tinted window, keeping my eyes on the house until it was far from my view, accepting that I would never see it again.

* * *

"Don't be afraid." Gilles' large hand covered mine where it gripped the arm rest. It was my first plane ride and the shaking of the large beastly machine frightened me a little.

"What is that?" I asked him.

"It's called turbulence. We're just flying

through a few rough pockets of air. But we're safe, so don't worry, okay?"

I nodded, turning my hand over and he smiled, cupping it between his. His hands were so big mine completely disappeared. "You been on a lot of planes?" I asked.

"I have."

"Is it like this every time? The rough spots, I mean."

"Just for a little bit. Then it stops." When I just nodded again, taking his word for it, he squeezed my hand and said, "You will love living with us. Mom decorated a room for you, and I put up a tree swing."

"Really?" I smiled, happy he would go through the trouble, and happy to know I was really wanted there and not just an obligation. "Will you push me in it?"

"Every day."

I stared at him for a moment, measuring his words in his expression. It brought to mind what Mama used to say to me. She always said I was very mature for my age and carried an old soul inside.

When I asked her why she said that, her answer was, "Because you are a deep thinker, my lady. Your golden eyes hint of much wisdom." I didn't know what any of it meant, but Mama was a wise woman herself. At least I thought so.

"What are you thinking about, pretty girl?"

I told him and he smiled. "I do believe your mama was right. Because I think you see me better than anyone."

Contemplating his words, I rested my head against his shoulder and closed my eyes hoping sleep would take me until we landed.

J. Adams

Chapter 2

Park City, Utah

My eyes grew large as we drove up the private drive leading to a huge log home surrounded by trees. The house was nestled beneath the snow-covered mountainside, and the view looked like something I had seen on one of those shows about rich families, the ones where you walked inside and everything was elegant and smelled new, with place settings on the table and furniture so clean and shiny, you didn't want to touch anything. And as we entered the house, I realized I wasn't far off. Tiled floors. A chandelier in the entryway. Leather furniture. Crystal vases on the mantles. Everything was exactly as I expected it to be, with the exception of the table being set. The one in the formal dining room was, but the high cherry wood kitchen table was bare except for a small green plant sitting in the middle. I really didn't want to touch anything.

"Welcome home," Marco said with a smile.

"Thank you."

"Let's go see your room," Gilles said, carrying my suitcase. I followed him upstairs.

Like everything else about the house, my room was large. Painted in beige, peach and purple, the bedding a combination of bright purple and peach floral and stripes, it was the nicest room I had ever seen. Stuffed animals and dolls filled two shelves and the tall corner bookcase held some of my favorite stories. A large, cream-colored plush area rug covered the dark hardwood floor. A flat screen television hung over the corner fireplace and the walk-in closet held new clothes for me, as well as some of my old ones. I even had my own bathroom.

"What do you think?" Gilles asked. "Do you like it?"

"Yes!" I turned to his parents. They had followed us up. "Thank you!"

Marco's pleased grin and Gina's reserved smile were their responses. "You two get your things put away as soon as you can," Marco told us. "We're going out for dinner." Then they left.

Gilles went to his room to unpack and I started putting my clothes away, unpacking some of the things that were sent the week before. I placed the photo of Mama, Daddy and me on the dresser along with a few others. The one Mama and I had taken together a few months before she died was precious to me and sat on the nightstand beside the picture Gilles and I took together the year before. That way, I would wake to see them each day. There was a keepsake box of letters Mama had written to me. Marco found them in one of her drawers when they were cleaning out her room. There had been a note attached that said, *'For Giselle.'* There were 25 letters and notes and I read all of them the day he gave me the box. I held the box close for a moment before placing it beneath the nightstand within easy reach.

There were other things. A watch that Daddy gave her and a book of her favorite poems. A gratitude journal. A set of silver beaded hair combs that she always wore on special occasions before her hair fell out from the chemo. A couple of classical music CDs and a book of old bedtime stories and nursery rhymes that she read to me every night when I was little. So many memories.

Sitting on the floor among the rest of Mama's things, a feeling of sadness swept over me. Wrapping one of her sweaters around me, I lay on the floor and cried, missing her so much, and missing the life I had to leave, the one I had with her. I closed my eyes and covered my face, rocking back and forth the way Mama used to rock me whenever I was feeling down. The sweater still smelled like her, like sunshine and warmth, and even a little Seattle rain.

A moment later I felt myself being lifted and was soon cradled in Gilles' lap.

"It's all right," he soothed. "It's going to be

okay."

Lifting my head I looked at him. He was the closest thing I ever had to a brother. "You won't ever leave me will you?"

I watched his smiling blue eyes tear up. "I promise I'll always be here," he said, wiping my tears away. "You couldn't get rid of me if you tried. Okay?"

I answered, "Okay," because I knew that's what I was supposed to say, but I wasn't sure about anything enough to believe it.

He kissed my forehead. "Come on, let's go. Mom and Dad are waiting."

I took his hand, he helped me up and we went downstairs.

J. Adams

Chapter 3

The ski resort town of Park City had a current population of 7,398–well, now that I was there make that 7,399. It had been founded as a silver mining town. Gilles told me it was where many of the wealthy now lived, which obviously included his family. Park City was also a celebrity hangout during certain times of the year, specifically during the Sundance Film Festival. I had never heard of it, but then again, I was just a kid. Still, I couldn't help wondering if we would see any celebrities. I asked Gilles what he thought and he said you never know.

Main Street was an uphill walk. The street was lined with shops and restaurants and looked like it stretched to the mountain. People wandered in and out of doors, some dressed in winter coats and hats, and some in only thick sweaters. It looked like a busy area, but Gilles said that was nothing compared to the summer.

We dined at an Italian restaurant. Marco, Gilles and I had pizza and spaghetti while Gina had Mediterranean chicken and a salad. Watching me eat, she commented that since I was a dancer I should eat better. Marco snorted and circled my tiny wrist with his thumb and pinky finger. They ringed my arm like a bangle bracelet. That stopped any further comments on my weight. Gilles squeezed my shoulder and smiled and I glanced at Gina again. I was only ten years old. Weight was the last thing I should have been worrying about.

I stated to wonder if this was how it would be with her and me. Would she expect me to be a perfect child? Would she try to mold me into her image? I sure hoped not.

"We'll get you enrolled in a ballet class on Monday after school," she finally said. And that was it. She said nothing else for the duration.

I was coming to find out Gina didn't talk much.

* * *

When we got back home, Gina said she was tired and was going to bed early. Like I always did with Mama, I wished her a good night. She said goodnight back, but there was no warmth in it. She seemed so different from the friend Mama described as being so much fun. It was like all the fun inside her had somehow dried up, and all I could think at the moment was how much I missed Mama's hugs and goodnight kisses. I wondered if the feeling of loss would ever fade.

Marco said he needed to do some paperwork and headed to his office, leaving us standing in the entryway.

"Come on," Gilles said, taking my hand. "I want to show you something."

We walked through the family room, which

was separated from the formal dining area by a tall stone fireplace that touched the ceiling. A retracting glass door reached across the entire area. He opened the door a little and we walked out onto an enormous deck overlooking a sloping yard bordered by trees. On the deck was an enclosed fire pit, surrounded by cushioned chairs and there was a hot tub in a corner. Turning on the lights, he led me over to the porch railing.

"Look," he said, pointing down into the yard and I grinned. There it was, just as he'd said, a swing hanging from a thick tree branch. "You can try it out tomorrow."

I hugged his waist. "Thanks, Gilles!"

"You're welcome, pretty girl."

I smiled, loving his nickname for me. I couldn't imagine anyone else calling me that.

We went back inside and played video games in the family room, ate popcorn, and talked about all the things we planned to do together. Gilles told me about the school I would be attending and how there was a dance studio a couple of miles away. A lady his mother knew owned it and had it built onto her home. He told me about some of his friends and asked me about the ones I left behind in Seattle. I was sad talking about the two good friends I had. Gilles cheered me up by assuring me I would make new friends that I would like just as much. And I also had him.

I asked Gilles if he had grandparents. He told me Gina's father died four years ago and her mother lived in Chicago. Gina and her mother had a falling out over something and haven't spoken in ten years. Sadly, Gilles had never gotten to know his grandmother. Marco's parents were both older when they had him and were gone now. He had an older sister living in Australia that he hadn't seen for years.

It was late when I finally got in bed. I had washed my face and brushed my teeth before putting my pajamas on, the same routine Mama taught me. Then I said my prayers, thanking God for everything I could think of, which usually took a while. Mama always said she was proud of me for not forgetting. I would never stray from that routine.

As I lay in the very dark room (no street lights were shining through the window like in Seattle) I thought about the de Francescos and my future with them. They were my family now. They were all I had. Mama must have felt sure they would take good care or me or she would never have asked them to. She trusted them and I had no choice but to look to them for my care. I had to trust that they would be good to me. I drifted to sleep with those thoughts.

But later in the night, I awakened to my own sobs, my pillow soaked with tears.

"Giselle?" Gilles' voice softly called in the darkness. He turned on the lamp and sat on the edge of the bed. His eyes were sleepy, his hair disheveled, his t-shirt rumpled. "Bad dream?"

"I don't know," I answered, wiping my eyes. "I'm sorry I woke you." His room was right across from mine.

"It's okay. Are you afraid?"

I nodded. "It's so dark here."

He left the room and came back a moment later with a nightlight and plugged it into an outlet across the room by the French doors. Beyond them was a small balcony with a pretty view during the day.

"How's that?" he asked, turning off the lamp. The small light illuminated the big room just a little.

"It's okay, I guess." I looked up at him, my eyes filling with tears.

His mouth turned up slightly in a sad smile. "You're missing your mama too, huh?"

I nodded.

"You want me to stay for a bit?"

"Could you? Just until I fall asleep."

"Yeah."

He grabbed a folded quilt from the foot of the bed. I scooted over and he stretched out on top of the blanket. Covering himself with the quilt, he leaned back against the headboard and wrapped an arm around me. I curled into him. Kissing my forehead he whispered, "Go to sleep. I'll be right here."

"Okay." After a moment I asked, "Do you think Mama can see me from heaven?"

"I do. I think she's probably watching over you now."

"Do you think it makes her sad to see me crying?"

"I think she understands. She knows you can't help being sad without her. She loves you a lot." He tightened his arm around me a little. "Personally, I think heaven is kind of close to us."

"Do you really think so?"

"I do."

"You don't think I'm being a baby, do you?"

"I don't."

"Promise?"

"I promise."

"You won't ever leave me, will you?"

"Never, my pretty girl."

Satisfied, I wrapped an arm around him, snuggled closer and closed my eyes, feeling totally safe. And as I drifted to sleep, everything inside me knew Gilles really would always be there.

Chapter 4

Six years later

"Ah, man, I'm looking forward to Christmas break!"

"So am I." I smiled at my friend Tanya as we took off our toe shoes. The teacher had us rehearsing overtime for the Christmas performance. We were doing Swan Lake and I would be dancing the part of Odette. Tanya would dance the part of Queen Mother.

I was in my senior year and looking forward to getting out of school for good. For me, twelve years was enough. Gina kept encouraging me to apply to

Julliard, practically scoffing at my dream of having my own dance studio. She was also pushing Gilles to go to college and do something more than body and engine work at his father's Park City foreign car branch. Gilles enjoyed his work and had no desire to change. At twenty-one he'd inherited a substantial trust fund and could really do whatever he wanted. And what he wanted was to eventually open his own shop. Like me, he had dreams that he held on to and nothing was going to make him give them up. I really loved that about him.

I sighed. Whenever I thought of Gilles, only one term came to mind: my best friend.

Through the years we grew to be as close as any brother and sister could be, yet for me it went so much deeper. Because of Gilles, I managed to survive the years without Mama and I learned to be brave. I supposed his courageousness rubbed off on me a bit. I learned so many lessons from Gilles. He taught by example, which made him loved and respected by everyone around him.

Don't get me wrong. We had our moments.

We had a few arguments here and there through the years that left me screaming and slamming the door in his face, but they were few and far between. I could never stay mad at him because he wouldn't let me. He was my light in the darkness. He had always been, from the moment I met him.

Marco was a loving father figure and I grew to love him as much or more than my own dad. As a matter of fact, he had become Dad to me and I started calling him that. No matter how busy he was, he always made time for me and placed importance on everything in my life. He encouraged me to do well in everything I attempted and to always follow my dreams. I think it was because he was such a dreamer himself. For a man who seemed to have everything, he spent a lot of time lost in his thoughts. Sometimes he would share them with me, other times they were his and his alone and I knew when not to intrude. He was such a good man.

Sadly, I learned to accept that Gina would always be Gina, and I think she liked it that way. In fact, she preferred that I keep calling her by her name.

She was there but not there, present in my life but aloof. There were scattered times when I earned her genuine praise and she really seemed to care. Like whenever I brought home my report cards. Just like Gilles, I was a straight A student. That made her happy and she always rewarded my academic efforts with material things, whether it be new clothes, shoes, or a day at the spa.

Each time I performed at a ballet recital and executed every move perfectly, I was praised and doted on in front of the other parents. I automatically latched on to that attention because I knew that once we were home again, things would be back to normal. Because of this, she would always be just Gina to me. Thanks to her, I developed a thick skin over the years where my emotions were concerned.

But Gilles could always pierce my armor. He could pierce it because he understood. He understood *me*. We were two of a kind, he and I, and his place in my life was permanent. He'd carved his initials there simply by being Gilles.

* * *

March 2006

"I've got a feeling you're going to make lots of new friends today."

"Maybe they won't like me."

"Yes, they will, and your teachers will love you. Just be your lovable self."

"You're the only one who thinks I'm lovable."

"Because you are."

Gilles held my coat while I slipped it on. His positive words did little to calm me. This was going to be my first day at Jeremy Ranch Elementary and I was beyond nervous.

"Are you ready?" Gina asked, handing me the lunch bag she'd packed.

"I guess so." I tried to smile, but it was more a wince.

"Let's go."

"Hey," Gilles said, catching my hand before I got in the car. "I want to hear all about your day later. And remember, just be yourself and it will be okay."

I smiled and nodded. At least sharing my experiences with him would give me something to look forward to.

* * *

And Gilles was right. It was an okay day. I managed to open up and talk to some kids, and I made a friend.

"Her name is Tanya," I told him as he pushed me on the swing. "We sat together at lunch. She's nice."

Gilles grinned. "See, I told you you'd make a friend. Who could resist that smile and bubbly personality?" His wide-eyed expression made me laugh.

Each and every day, even after a hard hour of wrestling practice, Gilles would arrive and I would immediately run to him. He'd catch me and kneel so I could hug him. Then he would push me in the swing and ask me about my day. He made the transition into my new life so easy. He made everything all right.

July 2006

It was our birthday. I turned eleven and Gilles sixteen.

Gina and Marco took us out to dinner. Afterward, we went home and had a small party. Gina had suggested that we have separate parties, but Gilles insisted we celebrate together. They had a large cake made with both our names on it and we received gifts– he from his friends and me from mine–and we got gifts from Gina and Marco. They gave Gilles a car and me a laptop computer.

When the party was over, Gilles went out with his friends. I sat at the desk in my bedroom where Marco hooked up the computer and set things up for me. He set the password, put on a web filter and showed me how to set up an email account.

Marco knelt beside my chair. "I know a computer isn't much compared to a car, but that will give you something to look forward to on your sixteenth birthday."

"I'm happy with my computer." I kissed his cheek. "Thank you."

"You're welcome." He caressed my hair. "You deserve so much. I'll do everything in my power to help you be happy here." He paused. "You are happy here, aren't you?"

I nodded. "I am happy being here with you. And Gilles."

"I'm glad. I know you probably still miss your mama sometimes."

I nodded. "But I have her letters and notes. They help me to not feel so sad."

"It's good she was able to write them. She loved you so much."

After sitting and talking with me for a short while, Marco left me with a kiss on the cheek and a final birthday wish. I thanked him again for the party and the present.

I tried out a few of the computer programs and finished setting up an email account, wanting to wait up for Gilles, but I soon grew tired and went to bed. Before I lay down, I glanced at the box of Mama's letters. Opening it, I took out the first one and read it again.

November 1, 2005

My Sweet Girl,

This is a bittersweet moment for me. I am

doing something that I should have started long ago. My time with you is growing shorter by the day, so I wanted to share with you some of my thoughts, as well as my hopes and dreams for you.

One of the promises I've made to myself is to make the most of each and every day I have left on this earth with you. So I am making notes and taking mental pictures of each moment I can, because they are all precious, and I will take those memories with me. You will keep them safe in your heart and know that whenever you are lonely, scared or sad, you can pull out these letters and little notes and know that I am near, loving you as much or more than I ever have.

Charlotte Bronte said, "The human heart has hidden treasures, In secrets kept, in silence sealed; The thoughts, the hopes, the dreams, the pleasures, whose charms were broken if revealed."

The quote may mean something to you when you're older, but what I want you to take from it now is though you won't see me, I'll never be far away. You can share with me the secrets of your heart, your hopes, and your dreams, and I will understand and keep them safe for you. Never forget that.

I love you, Giselle.

Mama

"Thank you, Mama," I whispered. "Thank you for being here for my birthday." I refolded the letter and placed it back in the box, returning it to its place under the nightstand. I turned off the lamp and fell asleep by the glow of the nightlight.

"Giselle," Gilles whispered sometime later. "Are you awake?"

"I am now," I whispered back sleepily and he chuckled softly.

He turned on the lamp and sat on the bed. "Sorry it took me so long to get back. We ended up hanging out with a few girls from school."

"So you were on a date."

"Well, I wouldn't call it a date."

"Were there as many girls as boys?"

"Yeah, I guess so."

"Then it was a date."

"Okay, okay, I guess it was a date then."

I smiled smugly about being right. "Did you have fun?"

"It was all right. I have more fun with you." He playfully tugged on a lock of my hair. "I have one more gift for you."

"Really?" I sat up and rubbed my eyes and he handed me a small box. I grinned when I read the top and quickly opened it. It was a charm bracelet. I had been looking at one in a fashion magazine a couple of weeks before and had even torn out the ad. Gilles saw it on my desk and asked me about it. I couldn't believe he actually bought it.

Between the colorful beads and silver spacers were five hanging charms: a silver pair of ballet shoes, a heart, a musical note, a book, and a flat round charm with the word *forever* engraved on it.

"It's so pretty!" I hugged him tight. "Thank you!"

"You're welcome, pretty girl," he said, hugging me back.

June, 2008

I was so proud of Gilles as he walked across the stage to accept his diploma. He was now a graduate of Park City High. At six-foot-four, he practically towered over most of his graduating class.

"What do you, think, pretty girl?" he asked me when he finally met up with us. He leaned down to accept my hug, holding me a moment.

"I'm so happy for you!"

"Thanks, me too."

We took some pictures and then had someone take one of all of us together.

Afterward, Dad and Gina allowed Gilles to have a party at the house and the place was packed. The food had been catered and was delicious. And what a variety! Mini hamburger sliders, buffalo wings, finger sandwiches, cheese and meat trays, hot and cold dips and chips, mini cheesecake squares, and a variety of brownies. It was a lot of food, but the guests plowed through it quickly.

I was only at the party for a short while when Gilles insisted that I go up to my room or just stay upstairs.

"You don't want me to stay?" I asked him.

"No, I don't."

Judging from his set expression, I think he expected me to argue, but I didn't. I guess he was too old to have me hanging around now. Gina told me it would happen sooner or later. She said I couldn't expect him to want me around as much because he was older and needed his space. I had never been clingy and had always given him his space just as he had given me mine. But now things were changing.

Suddenly, I wished I had agreed to the sleepover a couple of friends had invited me to. I'd said no because . . . because I thought . . . I don't know what I thought really.

Not allowing my hurt to show, I turned and went upstairs, leaving the noise behind. Closing my bedroom door, I changed into a t-shirt and shorts and put on my toe shoes. After rolling up the rug, I turned on the stereo and put in a CD I'd burned, then I danced. My room was so big there was plenty of room for me to move.

Shutting everything out, I became lost in the

music. The instrumental was by a local artist and it was one of my favorites. The music was versatile, changing from acoustic guitar and piano to a Scottish jig, then merging into an African rhythm mix, and finally fading into piano again. It was a beautiful piece of music. I had recorded the tune to play five times in a row before moving on to another song and I danced through them all. Exhausted, I finally stopped and turned the stereo off.

"You're amazing."

Gilles' voice startled me. I hadn't even heard him open the door. He was leaning in the doorway. "Thanks."

He entered the room. "Can we talk?"

"What about your party?"

"It's done."

"Already?"

"Yeah, I was tired and over it."

I sat on the bed and took off my shoes. "How was it?"

Sitting down next to me, he lifted my legs over his lap in a way that was routine and rubbed my feet.

"Not as great as I thought it would be, just loud. Of course, with Rick and Dean here, I didn't expect anything else."

I snorted, totally understanding what he meant. Rick and Dean had been his friends through all of high school and they got along great for the most part. They were also on the wrestling team and were obnoxious, but still good friends.

Then something changed between them. I never understood what happened. Maybe they just grew apart, I don't know. But things were not the same.

"I'm sorry if I hurt your feelings tonight."

"It's okay. I know I'm still young. Too young to be around you and your friends."

Gilles sighed. "Yes, you are young, but that's not why I didn't want you down there. The difference in our ages has never mattered to me. You know that. Besides, you're an old soul according to your mama, remember?" He laughed at my arched brow. I remembered well when I shared that with him on the plane. "No, Giselle, I had my reasons for not wanting you there. You see, even though you are only twelve, well, thirteen next month, you're a beautiful girl. You look older than you are and guys notice."

"But most of those people were strangers to me. They were your friends. They weren't paying any attention to me."

Gilles' expression was grim. "Trust me, they were. I know a few pretty well and I just didn't want you around them. They've already said some things that put me in the mind of hurting somebody. It wasn't you, Giselle, it was them. It was my way of protecting you. I know you don't understand, or maybe in a way you do."

And I did. "Are Rick and Dean the ones that said something about me? Is that why you guys aren't like you used to be?"

"I guess you are more aware than I thought. Yeah, they did say some things and I shut them both up, so don't worry about them or anyone else." He cupped my cheek with his hand. "You mean more to me than anything, pretty girl, and I'll never do anything to hurt you or let anyone else hurt you either.

Okay?"

His face was so serious, so sad. I didn't want him to be sad. I couldn't stand the thought of it. "Okay."

He smiled and it was like the sun coming out again. "All right. We'd both better get some sleep. Going to Disneyland tomorrow, remember?"

I gave him an excited grin. I had always wanted to go to Disneyland. Mama and Daddy wanted to take me but never got the chance.

"Goodnight, Giselle." He kissed my cheek.

"Goodnight."

After he left, I closed my eyes and let my thoughts drift back to when he and his family came to visit us in Seattle. One day Gilles walked with me to the park down the street from my house. It had started to rain (big surprise) but we stayed anyway. I was in one swing. Gilles was in the other. He had to hold his long legs up to keep his feet from scraping the ground with each pass. It didn't matter that we were getting wet, we just enjoyed our time together talking about all the things we loved about the rain. By the time we were done, our list was long.

A couple of the neighborhood boys walked over to the swings. They were older than me and liked to bully the younger kids. Whenever I was there and they came around, I usually went home to avoid being the target for the day. I had warned Gilles about them on our way there.

One boy began to kick mud in my direction, and just as the other put a hand out to pull a lock of my hair, Gilles stood. The boys quickly backed up, intimidated by his size. He told them if they didn't want to wind up in a world of hurt they should turn around and leave. The boys had looked at each other, then back at Gilles, like they were trying to decide if they could take him. But the look in Gilles' eyes made them rethink things and they started walking away.

He called after them, "Hey, just so you know, I will be here for a while. If she tells me you bothered her again, you can kiss your park days goodbye because I promise I will take care of you both."

They never bothered me again. Gilles became my protector that day. He was still being my protector.

* * *

"So, I'll see you tomorrow," I said to Tanya, drawing my thoughts back to the present.

"I'll see you. I'm sure Greg Hanes-slash-Prince Siegfried will be here with bells on, anxious to get on the stage with you. He sure enjoys every opportunity he can get his hands on you. How do you deal with him anyway?"

Without thinking, I answered, "I imagine I'm dancing with someone else."

"Oooo, so who is this Mr. Lucky and why haven't you told me about him?"

"Because he's only in my dreams, a figment of my imagination."

" Great. I thought I was about to hear something juicy."

"Sorry, nothing to tell. In any case, if Prince Greg tries what he did the other day when Gilles walked in, he will lose his hands, or a few fingers anyway."

Tanya laughed. "What I wouldn't give to have your gorgeous brother for my bodyguard, only not in the brother capacity." She winked, flipping her long blond hair over her shoulder seductively.

I just shook my head and smiled. "Bye, Tanya."

"Bye."

Stuffing everything into my bag, I went outside to wait for Gilles, my smile fading as I pondered Tanya's last comment. Her words had hurt more than they should.

In so many ways, Gilles had been my brother, but I stopped thinking of him that way years ago. The day I turned fifteen, he secretly became something much more.

July 2010

"So, you're going to a party tonight? But it's our birthday. I planned to take you someplace special."

Gilles was not happy with my sudden plans. "But why didn't you tell me? Tanya wants to go to the party, but she doesn't want to go by herself. Jenny Baker invited us. I wasn't going, but Tanya really likes Jenny's brother and is only going because he will be there."

"But didn't you tell her it's your birthday?"

"She knows, and she wouldn't have asked me to go with her if you and I had had plans."

"I didn't tell you because it was a surprise, Giselle. If I had, it wouldn't have been a surprise."

I hated the frustration I heard in his voice, but it bugged me that he couldn't understand. "I'm really sorry, Gilles, but I'm going with her. We can do what you had planned tomorrow, okay?"

"Fine."

It was only one word, but the disappointed resignation in it rang clearly.

Dad and Gina sang Happy Birthday to us, we exchanged gifts and had some cake then I went to change. A few minutes later, Tanya's dad honked his horn. When I exited the house, Gilles was in the driveway beneath the hood of his lifted truck.

"Gilles?"

He closed the hood and looked at me, a smile curving his mouth, but it didn't reach his eyes. "You look . . . very pretty."

I glanced down at myself. I was wearing a

light green, crocheted knee-length sundress with gold gladiator flats and a yellow sweater. Instead of wearing my hair pulled back like I normally did, I had left it down and it fell around my face and shoulders in shiny ringlets.

"Thanks," I finally said. I stood there for a moment looking at him, hurting inside because I knew I was disappointing him. "I'll see you later, okay?"

"Okay."

"You'll wait up for me?"

"Yeah, I'll wait."

By the time we reached Jenny's house, the party was in full swing. Like many of the homes in Park City, Jenny's house was built with a log exterior and it was huge. But even with its size, there were still enough kids there to occupy most of the areas of the house.

I followed Tanya through the crowd, saying hello to everyone while she discreetly searched for Jenny's brother, Sean. As much as I wanted to be there for her, my heart just wasn't in it. I'd left a big chunk of it at home. Deep down, I wanted to be spending my birthday with Gilles, not surrounded by fellow students whose only care at the moment was who was wearing what and which guys and girls looked the hottest. I didn't care about those things. I only cared that I disappointed Gilles, my best friend in the world. I was sick inside and just wanted to go home.

"Tanya, I don't feel so well," I said, pulling her aside. "Would you mind too much if I went home? You could hang out with Jenny."

"It's fine. You do look kind of out of it. You want me to call my dad?"

"No, that's okay. I'll call for a ride."

Finding a quiet area, I pulled out my cell.

"Gilles, could you come and get me?"

I heard him sigh into the phone. "I'll be there."

As I headed to the door Seth stopped me. He was Rick's younger brother and had been in some of my classes.

"I'm surprised to see you here," he said. "Didn't really take you for a party girl." He and his friend were wearing obnoxious grins.

"I'm not exactly a hermit."

"That's good to know. But you're not leaving now, are you? The party's just getting started."

"Yeah, I'm not feeling too well. See ya." I started to walk by, but he blocked my path. "I really need to go."

"Why don't you stay?" He moved a little closer, cologne permeating around him, a wide smile splitting his face. "I can make you feel better."

"I doubt that, but thanks for the offer."

"You sure about that?" He ran his finger down my arm, his touch making my skin crawl. I moved away, backing into his friend. Looking Seth in the eye, I said, "Don't ever touch me again."

He threw up his hands. "Whoa, Miss Stuck up. Whatever."

Not bothering to comment, I walked around him and heard them laughing, but I didn't look back.

I was sitting on the front steps when Gilles pulled up. He got out of the truck and met me as I came down the walkway.

"I'm so sorry," I said, blinking tears onto my face. I quickly found myself wrapped in his embrace, my face pressed to his chest, his in my hair.

"It's okay, pretty girl. I understand. I'm sorry for not telling you about my plans."

"You shouldn't have to be sorry," I said, pulling away, taking his hands in mine. "It's our birthday, for crying out loud! I should have known."

He chuckled. "Tell you what. Let's just always remember we have a standing date for our birthday, all right?"

"Okay."

We walked to the truck and he lifted me up on the seat so I wouldn't rip my dress trying to climb in. "I just wish I hadn't ruined everything."

"You didn't. Are you still up for going? We'll have to hurry and forget about dinner, but we can still make it."

I noticed he'd changed his shirt and was wearing one of my favorites, a light blue button down oxford. "Yeah, I'm good."

He handed me a small box. He'd always given me an extra birthday present. I opened it, smiling as I pulled out the silver heart-shaped locket. It had a small ruby on the front. Inside the locket was a picture of the two of us that we'd taken the week before in a photo booth at the mall.

I hugged him and kissed his cheek. "I love it. Thank you."

His eyes grew soft. "You're welcome."

Gilles took me down to Salt Lake City to see a movie theater showing of the Royal Ballet of London performing Swan Lake. We barely made it before the last trailer started, which happened to be the Royal Ballet's Romeo and Juliet. Thankfully, Gilles had already purchased our seats, so finding them was easy.

With my hand tucked in Gilles', I was completely entranced during the entire performance and thought it was the greatest thing I had ever seen. As it was ending, Gilles leaned over and whispered, "I want to watch you perform that one day. You would be the most beautiful Odette anyone has ever seen."

My eyes met his in the flickering light of the screen, glimpsing the raw sincerity in them. Taking in the warmth of his smile, something shifted inside me, and in that moment I knew nothing would ever be the same.

That night, I lost my young heart and became privy to a beautiful, terrifying secret, one that I would harbor in quiet desperation and never tell another living soul.

I had fallen in love with Gilles.

* * *

Snapping back to the present, I exited Lana's studio as Gilles pulled up in my car–my sixteenth birthday present. His smile was warm as he got out and opened the door for me. As I took his hand to get in, I thought of tomorrow's performance. While everyone else in the cast would be performing for the whole audience, I would be dancing only for him.

J. Adams

Chapter 5

Our production of Swan Lake was the ballet in four acts:

Act 1 begins at a royal court. Prince Siegfried is the heir to the kingdom and he must choose a wife at his birthday ball. Angry that he can't marry for love, the prince escapes into the forest at night. He spots a flock of swans flying overhead and goes after them.

ACT 2 starts on a moonlit night in the mountains. It is a wild place, surrounded by forest. There is a lake in the distance, with ruins on one side.

Siegfried aims his crossbow at the swans and readies himself for their landing by the lakeside. However, when one comes into view, he stops. Before him is a beautiful creature dressed in white feathers, more woman than swan. Totally captivated, the two dance and Siegfried learns that the swan maiden is the princess Odette. An evil sorcerer captured her and used his magic to turn Odette into a swan by day and woman by night.

A group of other captured swan-maidens attend Odette in Swan Lake, a lake that was formed by the tears her parents cried when she was kidnapped by von Rothbart, the sorcerer. When she tells Siegfried her story, pity fills his heart and he falls in love. Just as he begins to swear his love to her—an act that will render the sorcerer's spell powerless—von Rothbart appears. Siegfried threatens to kill him, but Odette stops him because if von Rothbart dies before the spell is broken, she would be trapped that way forever.

In **Act 3**, the Prince returns to the castle to attend the ball. Von Rothbart arrives in disguise with his own daughter Odile. She seems identical to Odette in every way, except she wears black while Odette wears white. The prince thinks she is Odette. He dances with her and tells the court that he intends to make her his wife. Only a moment later, the prince sees the real Odette and realizes his mistake.

In **Act 4**, Siegfried returns to the lake and finds

Odette, where she forgives him after his desperate apology. Von Rothbart appears and tries to pull the lovers apart. The two realize the spell can't be broken because of Siegfried's accidental pledge to Odile. In order to stay together, Odette and Siegfried kill themselves by leaping into the lake and drowning. This causes von Rothbart to lose his power over them, and he dies as a result.

The performance was a success. As we took a final bow before the curtain closed, I squinted against the bright stage lights, moving my searching gaze over the high school auditorium, wondering where my family was. I was anxious to see them, to see *him*.

They came backstage bearing roses and bestowing hugs. Gilles greeted me last, and I warmed as his gaze swept over me, his eyes finally meeting mine. "You were amazing." Then his arms came around me and I felt myself melting on the spot. The entire time, my heart was declaring, *It was for you. You were the prince that I danced with.*

"You look beautiful," he whispered against my ear and I fought to keep my eyes from slipping shut, lest Dad and Gina see emotions best kept hidden.

This was getting harder to do with each passing day. But I knew I would continue to lock my feelings away. I had no choice. They would never understand, and neither would he.

We stopped by an Irish pub, had a late dinner and went home. My body was exhausted, but my brain was in hyper drive and I couldn't sleep. I padded across the hall to Gilles' room. His door was cracked, his light still on. I knocked softly.

"Hey, can I come in?"

"Sure." He was sitting up in bed, leaning back against the headboard, a leather notebook and pen in his hands. He put them in the nightstand drawer. I sat on the bed next to him.

"Did you really enjoy the ballet?"

"Did I enjoy it?" His expression was incredulous. "I loved it! I loved watching you. You were indescribable. I couldn't take my eyes off you. I don't think anyone else could either."

"Did you get some good photos?"

"I did." He smirked. "That prince guy seemed to really be enjoying himself. Each time he touched you or even got near you, he grinned so wide, I thought his face would split. I don't think he could stop grinning even if you paid him."

I laughed. "Yeah, he's such a dork."

"Well, that dork had a few too many hands. I was seriously contemplating jumping on the stage, pulling his tights up over his head and introducing him to the world's most painful wedgie."

I covered my mouth and giggled. "That would have been something to see. And I don't doubt you could have done it, especially with those guns." My eyes casually moved over his sculpted arms and the large chest muscles stretching the faded green t-shirt. He was perfection. Absolute perfection, and for a moment, the need to claim him as my own was so strong, suppressing it was physically painful. I swallowed hard, willing the pressing tears to stay away.

"Hey, are you okay?"

"Yeah," I said, smiling quickly. "Just tired."

"You know, in some ways, the prince and Odette were like Romeo and Juliet. A tragic couple being kept apart, unable to share their love with one another. So desperate to be together they kill themselves."

"Hmmm, I guess they really are alike."

"I can understand the love, but not the destructive choice. Taking their own lives didn't guarantee they would be together. If anything, they would be even more separated."

"You're right." I smiled slightly. "It was depressing, I know. I'll try to make sure the next ballet I do has a happier ending."

"That sounds good to me. Though truthfully, it doesn't matter. I just love watching you dance."

My face warmed. "I like it when you watch me." For a moment his gaze pierced mine and I knew I needed to get out of there. "I'll see you in the morning." I leaned in to kiss his cheek in my usual way, fighting the longing to linger. He turned his face slightly and my lips met the corner of his mouth.

He smiled. "Goodnight, pretty lady."

Oh, I thought, heading to my room. *I am in so much trouble.*

Chapter 6

"Wake up, sleepy head. Merry Christmas!"

I smiled sleepily at Gilles sitting on the bed, then glanced at the clock. 6:00am, right on time. Gilles and I were always the first to get up on Christmas morning. We would rush down the hall and wake up Dad and Gina before going downstairs. Even as old as we were, this was still our routine.

"Come on," he said, taking my hand, pulling me out of bed.

"Just a sec." Rushing to the bathroom, I rinsed with some mouthwash and grabbed a scrunchie, pulling my hair up in a messy bun on the way down the hall. Gilles seemed even more excited than usual, which meant he must have gotten me something special. He loved giving me gifts. Of course, he knew material things didn't matter much to me anymore. Not that they really did before. But he knew I preferred things that came from the heart.

Gina always went down first to turn on the Christmas tree lights before giving us the okay to come down. She soon did and we were off.

I opened Dad and Gina's gifts first, saving Gilles' for last. From them I received more clothes, shoes, purses, gift certificates to the spa, a gift card to a natural bath and body shop, and certificates to the dance supply store. I thanked them both. They were always generous. Gilles received shirts, CDs, tools, cologne, a new pair of Ray Bans, and two pairs of Doc Martins.

Gilles and I gave Dad and Gina a certificate for a weekend getaway at a bed and breakfast, some restaurant certificates, and a large framed collage of family photos to hang in their room.

To Gilles, I gave a scarf that I crocheted, a new blue shirt (because the color matched his eyes) a scrapbook I had worked on for the past year, filled with pictures of the two of us, and a watch. He thanked me and I discreetly told him to turn the watch over and read the inscription.

To G., who is always there. Forever, G.

It was a simple inscription, really, one that needed not be private, but the look in his eyes when he raised his gaze to mine told me that the simple statement meant as much to him as it did to me.

"Thank you," he said again, putting it on. I watched him fasten the clasp, wondering if I only imagined him blinking back tears. He finally looked up with a ready smile. "It's your turn now." He placed a large wrapped box in front of me.

Gina stopped talking with Dad and turned her attention to us, her intent stare making me nervous about opening it for some reason.

"What in the world is in there, son, the kitchen sink?" Dad asked, teasing him.

"All kinds of surprises and hidden treasures,"

he said, watching me unwrap the box.

The box was a small wooden decorative trunk with Japanese cherry blossoms painted all over it. The clasp and hinges were gold-tone and my name was stenciled on the lid. Under my name on a gold plate was engraved in elegant script, Dream Box. My nervousness suddenly gave way to excited anticipation. I lifted the lid, fascinated by what the trunk held.

The first thing I pulled out was an elegant, sterling silver framed Royal Ballet playbill for Swan Lake. Dad whistled and my mouth dropped open. I blinked furiously at the tears blurring my vision. "How did . . . where did you find this?"

"Oh, believe me it wasn't easy."

I held it like a priceless treasure (because it was to me) and had a hard time putting it down.

"There's more in there," Gilles teased.

Gina asked to see the playbill and she studied it while I pulled out the other things. And Gilles was right. There were many treasures.

A copy of the Royal Ballet Swan Lake DVD,

the Royal Ballet Romeo and Juliet DVD, a calendar, a Romeo and Juliet ballet music CD, a collector's book on Rudolph Nureyev, a Royal Opera House scarf, an Opera House bear and tote bag. Every single gift was a treasure, but the final gift stole my breath and I couldn't stop the tears if I tried.

Beneath the other things wrapped in soft tissue paper lay a framed 11x13 inch photo of me as Odette performing an arabesque. It was a close up, so it was just me. Gazing at my expression in the photo, it was obvious to me that he'd glimpsed what I'd kept hidden. I had been immersed in the love I carried inside, and that moment had been for him. In that moment, I had given my all, baring my heart and soul for him alone, my very being stripped bare. If his eyes had truly been open he could have seen it all.

I finally lifted my gaze to him, but he wouldn't meet my eyes. He kept his own averted, as if they had something to hide.

Then I knew.

Placing everything back in the box, I said, "Thanks so much, Gilles."

Gina said, "Those things must have cost a small fortune, Gilles."

I heard him sigh. "It wasn't that much, Mom."

It was a lie, I knew, but it was the most touching lie I had ever heard. And it had been for me.

"Well," Dad cut in, "whatever the price, it was worth it because it meant so much to our girl." He pulled me close and kissed my cheek, adding, "Gilles knows her well."

* * *

As usual, we were stuffed after dinner, or at least three of us were stuffed. Gina's mealtimes were all about portion control, even during the holidays. I loved food and could never restrict myself that way. And since Gina finally stopped commenting on my eating, I guess she figured out that I didn't need to.

That afternoon while Dad napped and Gina did a session on the treadmill, I sat on my bedroom floor and pulled the gifts from my dream box to look through them again. Dad was right. How well Gilles knew me. Better than anyone else. He couldn't have thought of anything more perfect.

Leaning back against the bed, my eyes slipped shut as I remembered how he looked at me that morning and the feelings that passed between us. We both knew now, and there was no denying it.

But what now? I didn't know where to go next. I was still young, too young.

"What are you doing?" Gilles' voice startled me a little.

"Just appreciating the incredible Christmas gift someone gave me."

Grinning, he sat on the floor next to me. "You really like it?"

"I really *love* it. It's perfect."

"Are you sure? Because I can get a refund on everything except the photo if you want."

"Touch any of it and you die!"

"Okay," he said, laughing. "I believe you."

Gazing into each other's eyes, we both fell quiet. There were so many thoughts and emotions warring within me and I had no idea what to say. Taking my hand, he slowly laced his fingers through mine and drew me closer. Resting my head against his shoulder, my heartbeat sped up at the feel of his lips roaming over my brow.

"Oh, Gilles," I whispered with emotion.

"I know, baby," he murmured. "I know."

Chapter 7

Each day found me struggling more and more to keep my love for Gilles hidden. And it didn't help when he looked at me the way he did because his heart was always in his eyes. During the day, I could barely concentrate in half my classes because my thoughts were always on Gilles, but somehow I managed to keep my grades up. Whenever we were together, it was torture for both of us because we were not yet free to openly show each other how we felt.

During the times that Dad and Gina were out, we took advantage of every moment. At those times we gave into our need for the touch of the other. We could sit for hours just holding one another. Then they would return and the distance was between us again.

* * *

On one particular morning, Dad headed out early. He was spending half the day in Salt Lake. Gina had gone to workout with a friend. I still had twenty minutes until I had to leave for school. Those twenty minutes were spent in Gilles' arms, his lips raining gentle kisses upon my brow, the echo of how much he would miss me filling my ears. I loved having him hold me and I always felt like a little doll in his arms. Once again, a hint of frustration seeped into me when he avoided kissing my lips, but I decided he must have had his reasons. It was obvious to me that he was a passionate man. I felt that passion every time he even looked at me. I loved the feel of his arms around me, holding me tightly against him, and I relished the opportunities to bury my fingers in his soft hair and caress his face. He told me I had no idea what my touch did to him. I felt the same.

By the time I got to school, I had to take a

moment and psych myself up academically before I went in, because my insides were mush.

"Okay, something is definitely going on with you," Tanya said during lunch. I had been smiling without realizing it. I needed to stop thinking of Gilles at school–a feat that I knew was not possible.

"Nothing's going on," I lied.

"Come on, Giselle. Is it a secret crush? A boyfriend I don't know about? What? You're killing me here!"

"Okay, okay! There is someone that I really like, someone who is close to the family. But he's older and doesn't even know I exist." I sighed, adding a realistic effect to the lie. "He's just someone I daydream about every now and again."

"I can understand that," Tanya said, sighing dreamily. "I've had it for your brother bad, but I know he's out of my reach. And even though he's a great daydream–boy, is he ever a great daydream–I have my sights set on someone more obtainable, someone like . . . his friend, Rick. Or," She paused, looking across the lunchroom, "Rick's brother, Seth."

I swallowed back the revulsion rising inside me. "Seriously?"

"Yeah, they're both good looking. However, it will be hard catching Seth's eye when he obviously has the hots for someone who won't even give him the time of day." She looked at me pointedly.

"Because he's obnoxious and a womanizer. I could never go for someone like him."

"I know, but there is something about him and his brother that really draws me in."

"That's because you have a bad boy habit." I noticed she had started wearing even lower blouses and tighter pants, the designer sweaters and jeans fitting her toned dancer's body like a second skin. How grateful I was that her sights had never been completely fixed on Gilles.

She laughed. "This is true. But mark my words, one of them will be mine by the end of summer."

I shook my head, smiling at her determination. "Well, good luck."

* * *

That evening, Dad had a business acquaintance and his family over for dinner. George and Phyllis Kingston were decent people and I really enjoyed talking dance with Phyllis–she studied ballet when she was a young girl–but their son Quinton was a complete pain. I felt his intent stare for most of their visit. He was Gilles' age, but he was nothing like Gilles, and the looks he kept giving me were positively lecherous. He wasn't a bad looking guy, but he had a subtle bad boy look, the kind of guy Tanya would be attracted to. In fact, midway through the evening, I almost called Tanya to invite her over. At least that would have taken his attention off me. His blond hair was short and curly, and his gray eyes were sly, like there was something sneaky going on behind them. Yep, he was definitely Tanya's type.

Gilles stayed close to me. At any given time, I could glance at him and find him wearing the same tight expression, a subtle anger etched in his features that only I could make out. I put a hand on his back, discreetly caressing in an intimate way.

"I'm going to help Gina clear the rest of the

dishes," I quietly told him. Gilles nodded, watching me walk away.

"Your sister's gorgeous," I heard Quinton say. I took a stack of dishes to the kitchen, so I didn't hear Gilles' response.

Gina followed me, carrying the last of the food. "Quinton seems like a nice young man. He definitely seems interested in you."

"He's nice," was all I could think to say, though it left a bitter taste in my mouth.

"Since he comes from an affluent family, he's a good catch."

For someone who's fishing for bottom feeders, yeah.

"You're graduating soon. You should really start thinking about dating more."

Are you kidding me? Since when did you become Molly Mommy? I didn't comment and she started putting things away. "I can take care of that," I said.

I didn't expect a thank you, so I wasn't disappointed when I didn't hear one. She left to join her guests. They had all headed to the game room to play pool. Rinsing off the plates, I loaded the dishwasher, soaking in a moment of solitude. If I didn't know Gina would consider it rude and in bad form, I would have escaped to my room and stayed there until everyone had gone and I could be with Gilles. But I knew she would be upset so I stayed.

I had just finished wiping off the counters when Quinton approached. Turning my back to him, I rolled my eyes, wishing I had gone to my room after all.

"Need any help?" he asked. His grin was playful, sneaky.

"No thanks, I'm done."

He took an orange from the basket on the counter and rolled it around in his hand. "So, you're graduating, huh?"

"Yep." I opened the drawer and started straightening the silverware, even though it didn't need it.

He walked around the counter and stood so close, I had to move away a little. "I'll bet you've got guys all over the school dying to sample you, don't ya?"

Just being near him grossed me out. "I think you need to go back to your parents."

"Why? We're both adults. Okay, you're almost there. You're old enough. So what's the problem?"

"The problem is I don't like you, Quinton, so please leave me alone."

"You heard her."

I heaved a relieved sigh when Gilles entered, his anger apparent.

"Chill out. We were just talking."

"No, you were annoying her. She told you to leave. So am I, only I'm not saying please."

Quinton grinned. "Wow! Looks like there's more to you guys than meets the eye. I'm guessing this garden's already been raided. The flower has been plucked."

Before Gilles could take a step, I jumped between them. I felt the muscles in his chest flexing against my palm. He was past angry. "Gilles, just ignore him."

Quinton laughed. "I was right. You have been tappin' that, haven't you?"

Anger instantly sliced through me, and all my good sense flew out the window. I looked up at Gilles. "He's all yours."

The moment I moved away, Gilles' fist connected with Quinton's nose. Quinton landed on his back, blood gushing from his nose.

"Dammit! I think you broke it!" His voice was garbled.

"Good." Gilles hovered over him, dropping a dishtowel on his face.

"I should press charges," Quinton said, sitting up.

Gilles smirked. "Go ahead. While you're at it, you can tell them how you propositioned a minor. That should go over well, don't you think?" His eyes met mine, a hint of guilt in them, but his gaze said, *I know, I'm one to talk, but you're mine. Only mine.*

Quinton staggered to his feet, holding the blood-soaked towel to his nose. I felt a little sorry for him. Just a little.

"Maybe you should go to the hospital," I said. "Gilles, should I get his parents?"

"Yeah, probably." He stared at Quinton, his voice turning hard. "Stay away from Giselle." He pressed a gentle hand to my cheek. "Quinton slipped on a puddle of water and hit his nose on the counter."

I nodded and rushed to the game room, rehearsing the story in my head. I was pretty sure Quinton would go along with it. He had no choice.

"Mr. Kingston?" The older man was bent over the table, attempting a tricky shot. He made it.

"Yes?"

I quickly had everyone's attention. "Quinton had an accident. He slipped in the kitchen and hit his nose on the counter."

"Oh, my goodness!" Phyllis said, rushing to the kitchen, followed by everyone else.

Gina pulled my arm, halting me. "What happened?"

"Exactly what I said."

She stared at me like she knew I was lying, but she didn't say anything else. Giving me another long look, she hurried to the kitchen.

Dad apologized to them. Mr. Kingston assured him it was no one's fault and accidents happen. Wisely, Quinton agreed and said he should have been more careful. I noticed Dad's quick glance at Gilles. I was sure he knew there was more to the story, but he said nothing.

Only after the Kingstons were gone and Gina had gone to bed did Gilles tell Dad the truth. Dad was livid, not at us, but at Quinton. He said he probably would have done the same thing, and he agreed with Gilles about Quinton not pressing charges. He hated that it happened, but he was glad Gilles was there for me. He kissed my cheek and said goodnight to us.

Later that night, Gilles held me, whispering into my ear over and over, "I can't stand the thought of anyone else touching you. I don't want anyone touching you."

I shushed him, caressing his face. "No one will," I promised. "No one but you. Only you."

J. Adams

Chapter 8

Winter merged into spring and the snow on the mountains slowly began to melt. The love between Gilles and me was ever-changing like the seasons, growing stronger and deeper with each day that passed. Then June came and graduation was upon me.

The ceremony was amazing because Gilles was there. Even though I couldn't see him, I felt his gaze amid the sea of faces swimming before me as I walked across the stage to accept my diploma. The hugs I received afterward from classmates, and even Dad, faded into oblivion the moment Gilles' arms went around me. I knew he would always affect me that way.

I was invited to a few parties, but I declined, and I opted out of having my own. I had no desire to spend the night surrounded by a crowd of people. There was only one person I wanted to be with–the most important person in the world.

It was on graduation night that Gilles kissed me for the first time. Dad and Gina had gone to bed and we sat out on the back deck. The sky was clear and full of stars, the light of the full moon illuminating the valley beyond us.

Gilles drew me down the steps into the back yard. He led me behind the large tree my swing still hung from, and then it just happened. He held me close as his mouth came down on mine, his kiss at first light and gentle, as if to test the waters. Then passion quickly seeped in, and before we knew it, we were practically devouring each other. He whispered of his love for me over and over and I did the same, our lips separating for the briefest of moments, the heat from our affections surrounding us, the taste of one another becoming an addiction.

Now I understood why he'd never kissed me before. With the feel of his solid body pressed against mine, his hands exploring my curves, my hand lost in his hair, the other sliding beneath his shirt, caressing his back, and his tongue sensuously rolling over mine in complete abandon, I had now stepped into womanhood, the innocence of youth left behind me. My eyes were open now and I truly understood. We could never step back now, only forward.

But how *could* we move on? Dad and Gina would not understand. Would they try to stand in our way?

Breaking the kiss, I pressed my face in the curve of his neck, breathing him in. His scent had become life to me. "Oh, Gilles," I whispered. "What are we going to do?"

Drawing back a little, he reached into his pocket and slipped a ring on my finger. He held me close again, our melded bodies cloaked in darkness. "Go on loving is what we'll do, even if it is in secret for now." He moved his lips to my ear. "We will have a life together. A life full of love and hope, a life that will be ours alone, where no one can separate us." His words were soft, strong, and passionate.

I fingered the diamond I had yet to see. "But Gilles, I'm so afraid that . . . that when Dad and Gina find out, they won't want anything else to do with me. And Gina will probably accuse me of seducing her son."

He snorted. "You seducing me? Enticing me maybe, but–"

"You know what I mean."

"Yeah, I know what you mean, but I think after a while, they will come to accept it."

I was too afraid to take that chance. Maybe after a little time passed, I would find my courage.

As perceptive as ever, Gilles pressed his lips to mine whispering, "It will be our secret until you're ready."

Gilles was so beautiful, both inside and out, and I felt blessed to lay claim to his heart. "I can't believe you really want to marry me."

He kissed me. "Why can't you?" he whispered

against my lips. "It had to be you." His warm mouth traveled to my neck, his lips moving to my shoulder, sensuously caressing, and I sighed at the sensation rippling through my body. Taking his face in my hands, I kissed him, taking control and he groaned, holding me tighter to him, the passion roaring between us threatening to set the tree aflame. We finally drew apart and just gazed at one another. Then, like the pull of a magnet to metal, we came together again, whispering, "I love you" over and over.

J. Adams

Chapter 9

The next day, Dad informed us that he and Gina had to take a spur of the moment business trip and would be gone for a week. They were going to acquire more cars for his Salt Lake lot. He said they really needed this little vacation.

As he spoke to us about the trip, all I could think of was we would have the whole place to ourselves for a week. A whole week! We wouldn't have to hide our feelings and could freely express what we vowed to keep secret. It would be a dream come true.

That day, Gilles was periodically deep in thought, and he left for a while, but he was back in time for us to take Dad and Gina to the airport.

On the way, Gina instructed us on taking care of the house. She still treated us like children. Well, she still treated *me* like a child. She had no idea how much I had grown up over the past year.

Once they were checked in and through security, we waved goodbye and walked hand in hand to the escalator and back up to parking. When we got in the car, he didn't start it right away. Turning in his seat, he took my hands and held them firmly, his blue eyes intent.

"Okay," I finally said. "You've got to tell me what's wrong." He opened his mouth to say something then stopped. "Gilles, you know you can tell me anything." I caught the indecision in his eyes, a look of worry creasing his handsome brow. "What is it?"

"I love you, Giselle. More than anything, more than my own life."

"I love you too."

He paused, continuing to stare, his gaze

roaming over my face. He started to speak again but hesitated.

"What is it?"

His eyes finally fixed on mine and held. "I want to marry you."

"And I want that too." I glanced down at the one-carat solitaire on my finger and smiled. "We are engaged, aren't we?"

"I want to marry you now. Today." I was at a loss for words and he pressed on. "You won't be eighteen until next month, which means we can't legally marry, but we needn't wait."

We watched a couple walking by our car. They stopped a few cars away and kissed. She was pregnant and he was dressed in a business suit pulling a suitcase. It looked like she'd just picked him up after a long separation.

"I've been giving this a lot of thought," Gilles continued. "I know someone. His family moved away during our senior year and he just moved back to Park City a month ago. He's . . . he is a minister. I explained our situation to him, and he said he would marry us. And though our marriage would not be legally recognized, it would be recognized to God.

"Then, next month on our birthday, we can get a license and marry again at the courthouse." He squeezed my hands. "I feel that we need to do this, especially spending a week in the house alone with the way we feel about each other. Before God and in our hearts we will already be married. The other will only be a technicality." He studied my face. "What do you think? If you tell me it's crazy, then we will wait. But everything in me is saying this is right."

All my thoughts finally passed through my lips. "I want to marry you today. There is nothing I want more."

He heaved a relieved sigh. "So you're good with it? With everything?"

"Yes," I answer with all the conviction in my

heart. "I'm fine with everything."

Caressing my cheek, he kissed me. "I love you, pretty lady."

"I love you."

J. Adams

Chapter 10

Later, I went through the house looking for Gilles, but I couldn't find him. His truck was still in the garage and he hadn't taken my car. I finally went down to the back yard, surprised to find him sitting beneath the swing tree. His head was resting in his hands, his knees drawn up.

"Gilles?" He looked up, but I couldn't read his face, his expression was completely blank. "Are you all right?"

Instead of answering, he stretched out his legs and pulled me down on his lap. I draped my arms around him and rested my head against his shoulder. Our surroundings were quiet, peaceful. A deer wandered into the yard. We usually had one or two walk through and nibble on the plants. Gina decided it was futile to try to stop them, so she stopped planting a garden altogether and replaced the flowerbeds with gravel and fake flowers. She covered them in the winter and surprisingly, they always looked great.

After holding me for some time, Gilles stood and helped me up. Only then did he speak.

"When I asked you to marry me today, I . . ."

"You what?" I pressed, fearing that he had changed his mind. Not only about marrying me, but about being with me, period. Maybe he'd decided it wasn't worth it. I didn't think my heart could handle that.

"I feel like I pushed you into saying yes today. I was being selfish. Our relationship is not about what *I* want. It can't be just about me. A marriage takes both people, and if one begins to dominate at the start, then there is no hope for real happiness." His gaze moved past me, settling on the swing. "From the moment I met you, you have meant everything to me. I promised to never hurt you and I want to keep that promise. I don't want to rush you into anything. You've probably dreamed since you were a little girl of having a big beautiful wedding with family and friends there, lots of flowers and a big cake." There was so much pain in his eyes he couldn't mask it. "I don't want to take those things away from you. I was totally prepared to do that today, but–"

"Can I talk now?" I blurted, surprising him. He nodded. I squeezed his hand, marveling that something so large and strong could be so gentle. "I have had two major dreams in my life–to own my own dance studio and teach, and to marry you. When you proposed last night, my biggest dream came true. And I will still have my own studio, just as you will soon have your own auto shop. Whether we marry now or a year from now, that will never change. As for a big wedding, I've never dreamed of that. I guess I'm not like other girls that way." He smiled. "I don't need a fancy gown or flowers or all the pomp. Nothing would be more perfect to me than just the two of us, baring our hearts and souls to each other and God. If I desired those other things, I would have to marry someone else, not the man everyone sees as my brother. I would rather tie myself to you, in every way possible." I caressed his cheek. "I want to marry you today, Gilles. I love you. You are my dream."

He held my palm to his mouth. "Are you sure?" His voice was rough with emotion.

"Do you love me?"

"With everything that I am."

"I am sure."

* * *

I was wearing a white sundress, Gilles a white shirt and khaki trousers. My hair was down and unadorned and the only jewelry I wore was the locket he had given me for my fifteenth birthday and my engagement ring. Our feet were bare, our hearts full, our eyes brimming with love.

Facing one another on the deck, bathed in the evening light, we vowed before God to love and treasure one another forever. Reverend John (this was what he asked that we address him by) witnessed our vows.

As Gilles spoke, I took in the contours of his perfect face. A five o'clock shadow had grown in and a lock of his tousled black hair fell against his forehead. He eyes were bright as they met mine.

Opening the Tiffany's box–the same kind of box my engagement ring came in, which would explain where he went earlier in the day–we slipped the platinum bands on each other's finger. Then Reverend John pronounced us man and wife and we kissed, knowing God was pleased with us because He had been a part of our union.

* * *

It was almost morning before we drifted to sleep, our energy spent from the intimacy we'd shared far into the night. I knew his touch now as well as he knew mine and we were of one mind.

His hands on my body had been indescribable. His fevered kisses, the very taste of him, his mouth, his skin . . . oh, heavens, I couldn't even think! It was intoxicating, consuming. His love was life to me, filling all my senses. He was heaven, a place in which I wanted to live forever and never leave. I knew he felt the same.

So how could a love so strong and deep and powerful be wrong?

Just on the edge of sleep, I asked him, "What will we do if no one accepts us?"

Holding me against the warmth of his body, he sleepily replied, "They will. If not, then we will live somewhere else."

* * *

The next morning we cooked breakfast together, laughing and talking while I flipped pancakes and he fried bacon and cooked scrambled eggs. This carefree time was both savored and deeply treasured.

After cleaning up the kitchen, we put on our swimsuits and lounged in the hot tub on the deck. Since we were unable to keep our hands off each other, we were glad our home was so secluded. The only witnesses to our affections were the birds and maybe a few farsighted deer. We stretched out on a couple of beach towels and dried in the sun. By noon, we went back to bed, made love again and napped for a long while.

That evening, Gilles grilled steaks and I made a salad. I loved just watching him. The yellow t-shirt hugged his astounding physique and the denim shorts showed off his perfectly toned calves. I couldn't believe he was really mine.

We ate dinner outside. A feeling of contentment swept over me as we watched each other, absorbing the fact that we were married. The warmth of his gaze reflected our new level of closeness. I still pinched myself at times to make sure I wasn't dreaming. With just the two of us there, I could pretend that it was our house, and that we were just like any other couple. I was a loving wife, caring for our home and dreaming of the future.

Then I would come back to earth and remember that we were not like any other couple. We couldn't go out and act like we were bound to each other, a fact that hurt to think about. So I decided *not* to think about it and just enjoy what we had.

"Hey," Gilles said, taking my plate and placing it on the table. "I love you."

I smiled. "I love you too."

He kissed my hand. "Everything will be okay. I promise."

Chapter 11

"So I've been thinking about where to take you for a honeymoon."

"Really?" I stretched out, lying across his chest. It was noon and we still hadn't gotten out of bed. Outside, heavy drops of summer rain fell and I could smell its crispness, the scent carried through the open window by a gentle breeze.

"Yeah, we definitely need a honeymoon. We can leave on our birthday right after our courthouse visit. Where would you like to go? We can go anywhere."

"Anywhere?"

"Yep."

"When I was younger, I dreamed of traveling to Verona and seeing the home of Juliet."

"That would be Casa di Giulietta."

"Ah, I love the way you say it. So Italian."

"That's because I'm half Italian," he said, tickling my ribs and I giggled. "I was born in Rome, remember?"

"I almost forgot."

"Would you really like to go to Verona?"

"I would love it, but how? What would we tell Dad and Gina?"

"We can tell them I'm taking you to Italy for a graduation gift."

"What if they decide to go with us?"

"I don't know. We'd figure it out. Let's just hope they won't." He sighed. "Giselle." He softly rubbed my back. "Baby, we're going to have to tell them eventually."

Pressing my face against his chest, I released a sigh of my own. "I know."

He tightened his embrace. "They will accept

our marriage. They'll have no choice."

* * *

It was our last day alone.

When we got up, Gilles made the travel arrangements. He purchased our plane tickets and rented a small villa in Verona not far from Juliet's castle. He had traveled to Verona when he was nine and only remembered a little about it, so he was excited to take me and revisit the city. There would be no time for me to get new credentials, so I would have to use my current license and passport. We would fly out on the evening of our birthday.

We spent the rest of the day making sure the house was in order, cleaning, dusting and sweeping the floors. Not that we really needed to do much. We just didn't want to give Gina anything to complain about. We took every opportunity to hold one another and just be. Things would be different when they got back. We would have to act different, something I was definitely not looking forward to. And the thought of not sharing a bed was painful for us both. I was sure I would find my way to his side during the night or he to mine. We'd slept in my bed the entire time because he liked that it smelled of me. Somehow we would find a way to be together.

That night we made love again and again, not wanting to sleep until we had to, because we knew when we awakened, the dream would need to be put away.

Chapter 12

When we picked our parents up, our fingers were bare, our wedding rings tucked away in the bottom of my dream box.

Despite Dad rattling off the details of their trip, the ride home was a solemn event, Gilles and I wanting nothing more than to be alone again. Nevertheless, we filled the bouts of silence with questions about Boston, trying not to give anything away. I only prayed that our eyes would not reflect the change in our relationship, that the longing looks would not betray us and tell of intimacy shared.

Gina asked, "So what did you two do while we were gone?"

Gilles answered, "The usual, watched movies, played games, beat each other up. Same stuff we always do."

Dad laughed, but Gina didn't. And I felt her eyes boring through the back of my head.

"We grilled some steaks," Gilles continued casually. "Turned out perfect. You would have loved them, Dad."

"I'm sure. You'll have to do a repeat."

"No problem."

A drive had never seemed so long and I was anxious to get home. When we arrived, I welcomed them back once more and went up to my room.

Glancing in the bathroom mirror, I wondered if I looked different, if the transformation from girl to woman showed. I prayed that it didn't, at least not right now.

Closing my eyes, I lowered my head and took a deep cleansing breath, telling myself everything was okay, that I was okay. *Oh, Mama, I wish you were here to talk me through this.*

Gilles walked in. "Mom just left to get her nails done. Dad is in his office."

He wrapped his arms around me from behind and held me close as we stared at our reflection. My husband was painfully handsome. His hair was tousled as usual, his blue eyes hypnotic. Though I paled in comparison, we looked good together.

"You're so beautiful," he breathed, his face pressed into my hair. "The most beautiful woman in the world. There are probably a thousand guys in this city who would love to be in my place right now."

"And probably just as many women who would kill to be in mine."

I turned in his arms, pressing my face in the curve of his neck, breathing in his cologne. I left a trail of kisses from his neck, along his jaw, then back down along the collar of his shirt. His embrace tightened, an emotional moan escaping him.

"Giselle," he groaned in my ear.

That one word said everything. I soaked it in, taking what I could, because each stolen moment was so precious. We kissed then, traveling again to our private haven, if only for a moment.

* * *

After Gilles left, I sat on the bed for a while and pondered things as they were. Thinking on Mama's letters, I pulled out the last one she wrote and read it again. The words meant more now than they ever did before.

My Sweet Girl,

This letter is a struggle to write, because I know it will be the last. There are so many things to say, so many things I want to tell you about life. But I don't have the strength—or the knowledge—to write them all, so here are the most important ones. These things will mean more to you as you get older.

First, let integrity encompass your entire being. Albert Einstein said, "Whoever is careless with the truth in small matters cannot be trusted with important matters." None of us can reach our full potential without integrity. Be truthful in all you do. I am inspired to tell you that there is a time to speak and a time to remain silent, but even in those times, let integrity rule.

Second, always seek after knowledge. You never want to let someone else do your thinking for you. As you grow, knowledge will eventually bring wisdom.

Third, never let go of your dreams. They will change as you get older, but never be afraid to go after what you truly want.

Fourth, don't ever be afraid to love. Love with your whole heart and soul. And when you finally meet the person you are meant to spend forever with, love him with all that you are. God will point you to the man worthy enough to hold your heart, and he will be a better man because of your love and presence in his life.

Have compassion for others and show you care.

Don't take offense too easily.

Respect others and yourself.

Live your life in a way that will cause those around you to be grateful they know you.

Finally, live your life, Giselle. Have the

courage and the faith to live.

I love you so much, my sweet girl. Always remember that.

Refolding the letter, I wiped my eyes. "I'm working on the courage, Mama. I'm working on it."

Chapter 13

The days passed slowly. Gilles kept busy doing engine work and body detail in the extra detached garage he'd turned into a temporary shop. I spent time each day helping Lana at her dance studio. Other times, I closed my bedroom door and I danced. I was able to keep up my skills, stay agile, and work off the frustration of not being with Gilles.

Sometimes though, he would slip into my room and watch me dance. At those times the look in his eyes stirred me so much, a heady shiver would run through me, affecting me as if he'd touched me. And oh, how I missed not having his touch whenever I needed it, which, of course, was all day every day.

"There's nothing more beautiful than watching you dance."

"I love having you watch me," I always said, my face growing warm each time.

He would only stay for a few minutes and our conversations were always about basic things, just in case Gina was roaming around, which she tended to do.

After midnight, I would go to his room or he'd come to mine. We'd lock the door, make love and sleep until five, then go back to our respective room and sleep a little longer. I hated not waking up next to him and he felt the same. Still, we held on. As much as I wanted go ahead and tell Dad and Gina about our marriage, something kept holding me back. Maybe it was just my fear, I don't know, but it was something.

I spent a lot of time reading up on Verona and Venice, looking at photographs, and reading the ratings and reviews of other travelers. Gilles wouldn't show me pictures of the villa because he wanted it to be a surprise, but he did list some of the amenities.

A few days before we were to leave, we told Dad and Gina of our plans. Gilles told them the trip was a graduation present from him. Dad thought it was a great idea. Gina didn't. No surprise there. She didn't really say much to either of us for the rest of the day. I've never understood how a person could be so distant, even after living under the same roof with her for so long.

* * *

The day before our secret courthouse marriage and departure, we were sitting at the table finishing up dinner when Gina said to Gilles, "Italy is an extravagant present. If you keep spending money the way you have been on her, you will run through your trust before you're twenty-five."

I bristled and Gilles squeezed my hand under the table. "Mom, for the most part, I am very frugal with my money, so if I want to spend it on things for Giselle, I do. Thanks to a few pointers from Dad, I've done well with investments and I'm secure."

"Why Italy of all places? Why not someplace

in the country? It would be cheaper."

"Because, Mom," he spoke through gritted teeth, "it's where she wants to go, and it's my money."

Dad spoke, his voice hinting of frustration. "Gina, they're adults. It's his money and he can do whatever he wants with it."

"It's always about her, isn't it?" She spat out 'her.'

"Yes, it *is* about Giselle," Gilles said, anger creasing his brow. "It's a graduation gift. It's where I want to take her."

I was used to the way Gina treated me and it seemed that the tension between us had been building for a while, but this new vehemence was puzzling and I couldn't help wondering if she knew about us. Choosing my words carefully, I finally spoke up.

"Gina, I'll always be grateful for the life you and Dad have given me, but I have always felt there was something about me that made you keep your distance. From the beginning I have gotten mixed signals from you. I've never really known how you felt about me. I have tried to be a good daughter. I'm not perfect, but I've tried. I just don't understand what I have done to earn your disdain today. Please tell me." I hated the desperation I heard in my voice, but any pride I harbored was gone.

Dad came to me and took my hands in his. "You haven't done anything, honey. Gina loves you."

"Do I?" she cut in, her voice bitter. Walking over to the kitchen window, she stared out at the mountains, her back to us, and released a deep breath. "Your mother was the best friend I'd ever had, next to Marco. I loved her like a sister, loved her more than my own sister. We met in junior high and were roommates in college. She helped me through some trying times when we were younger. She and Marco were the two people I trusted most in the world." She turned, fixing her gaze on me, her voice suddenly hard. "Until they betrayed that trust."

Dad moved toward her. "Gina, don't do this."

"Why? She asked, didn't she? She wanted to know the truth. Now she will."

"This is only your version of the truth, not–"

"It's the only truth, Marco!"

He looked at me and sighed with a slight shake of his head, pain etching his features. Gilles reached for my hand and pulled me close, his expression telling me he was just as confused as I was.

Gina continued. "When we came to visit right after your father died, my heart ached for Adesina. Suddenly there she was, left alone to raise her child. I couldn't begin to imagine what she was going through, but I was glad we could be there." She paused, looking at Dad. He stood away from her, his hands stuffed in his pockets, his face expressionless. "It had just started raining again and you two were at the park. I couldn't find your dad and I figured he must have gone out for a bit and forgot to tell me. I had been helping Adesina with the laundry so I went down to the basement to put in another load. As I was coming down the stairs I heard soft voices. I walked around the corner to discover the two of them. He was holding her and she was clinging to him. He kept crooning to her, "I'm here. It's okay, I'm here.""

Dad shoved a hand through his hair. "Dammit, Gina! Why do you keep making more of it than it was?

I told you over and over there was nothing going on. She broke down and I was comforting her. End of story."

"It *was* more, Marco! You didn't comfort me like that when my sister died a few months later!"

"Because you wouldn't let me! You were so cold I couldn't get near you! I still can't!"

"Because you lied to me! You're still lying. I wasn't blind. I know what I saw. You had feelings for her. That's why you agreed so readily to take Giselle in. I guess if you couldn't have Adesina, you could at least have a part of her."

"Good grief, woman! She was your best friend! She was my friend! Yes, I cared about her, but you're my wife. I have always been faithful to you because I love you. I would never do anything to hurt you."

"But you did. I saw how she looked at you, how you looked at each other. And I saw the way you both looked at me. Like you had been caught doing something wrong."

"You looked at *us* like we were doing

something wrong. You didn't say anything, but your eyes said it all. You condemned us with a look."

"You condemned yourselves. And you continued to do so through the remainder of the visit. Glancing at her when you thought I wasn't looking. And her watching you, then darting her eyes away before I could catch her."

"Woman, you are being ridiculous! She was our dear friend. There was nothing. There could never be anything between us. Never, Gina!"

Gilles and I stood in silence, completely confounded by what we'd just heard. I watched a peculiar look pass between the two, but it was over in an instant. Gina finally looked at me again, her eyes devoid of warmth.

"So now you know. Now you know why you will never be more to me than you are."

Gilles put his arm around me, holding me protectively against his side.

"Your problems with Dad are not Giselle's fault. You have no right to blame her."

"Well, she is her mother's daughter, isn't she?

The same blood flows through her veins."

The tears I fought so hard finally burst forth, hot and streaking my face. "I'm sorry."

Dad came and enfolded me in his arms. "Don't you dare apologize. You have nothing to be sorry for. This has nothing to do with you."

"Oh, it has everything to do with her. As I said, she is her mother's daughter and . . ."

"And what?" Gilles asked, his voice like ice. "What were you going to say, Mother?" He waited but Gina said nothing. He grabbed my hand. "You know what? We're leaving tonight. We'll stay at a hotel."

"What about your birthday?" Dad asked.

"Don't worry about it, Dad. We'll make it up with you when we get back." I noticed he didn't include Gina.

Gilles led me upstairs, leaving Dad staring after us. My thoughts were jumbled and I was still trying to figure out what just happened. Since our bags were already packed, we just grabbed a few toiletries and our laptops. Within a couple of minutes we were ready. Gilles carried our bags out to the car then came back inside for me. I was checking my purse, making sure I had everything, including my passport when Dad came in. He handed me a folded check.

"What is this?"

"This is the money from your trust. I want you to have it now instead of waiting until you're twenty-one."

I was so surprised I didn't even look at it. "Why, Dad?"

"I have my reasons. I think you're mature enough to handle it. Open a new account tomorrow and deposit it. You'll be eighteen so you won't need us." I couldn't tell him Gilles had already added me to his so I didn't need another account. He hugged me, and then Gilles. "Have a great time and be careful."

"We will, Dad."

He walked us out. "Take care of her," he said to Gilles before we drove away.

"I will. I promise."

Chapter 14

That night, Gilles held me while I cried. Hearing what Gina really thought of Mama and me was the most painful thing I had experienced since losing Mama. All this time, she had been holding something she thought happened between Mama and Dad against me. My heart ached. Gilles told me he didn't believe it, that it couldn't be true. He trusted Dad. So did I.

Gilles rocked me and whispered over and over that he loved me. Then he made love to me and helped me forget for a while. I woke throughout the night as bits and pieces of the conversation went through my head over and over. Gilles' arms were always there to comfort and ease the pain enough for me to drift back to sleep.

The next morning we went to the courthouse, got a license and were married. Now, in the eyes of the world we were legal, though the vows Gilles and I made before God seemed more real. They meant more.

Afterward, we stopped by the bank and deposited the check into our account. I gasped when I finally looked at the amount. I had never seen so many zeros at once. Gilles just chuckled at my reaction because he had received the same.

We headed to the airport, parked in the long term lot and caught the shuttle bus. We checked in, and after passing through security, grabbed a quick bite to eat. An hour later we were boarding.

My fingers were laced through Gilles as we took off, and I couldn't help remembering my first flight to Utah. He'd held my hand then, too. Fingering my wedding rings, he smiled. No matter what happened, the rings would not come off again.

Staring out at the darkening skies, my thoughts drifted once again to what Gina said about Mama and Dad. In my heart I knew they were innocent and hadn't done anything wrong, but I couldn't shake the feeling that there was more to the story than we'd heard. We would probably never know and I didn't know if I even wanted to. After talking with Gilles for a while the night before, I knew he believed Dad too. In fact, he told me he was more inclined to believe his dad over his mom anyway. He was saddened by that fact, but he couldn't change the way he felt.

I had never been so hurt before. It would take a long time to fade, but I made up my mind about one thing. I wouldn't waste another tear on Gina. I had already wasted too many. I suddenly didn't care what she thought anymore.

But I did care about what Dad thought.

Resting my head against the seat, I turned to Gilles, staring at his profile as he looked straight ahead. He was relaxed, his seat reclined. He'd gotten us seats in first class, so there was plenty of room. He was immersed in his own thoughts. I squeezed his hand and reclined my seat back to the same level.

"Tell me again it will be okay."

He drew me close and I lay my head on his shoulder. "Everything is going to be okay. I promise."

* * *

Gilles

Gilles Antonio de Francesco was absolutely certain about three things:

First, there was a God.

Second, that God placed Giselle in his life because they were destined to be together.

And third, if he had to live without her, he'd be lost.

He loved Giselle so much it hurt. From the moment he'd met her, even at their young ages, she had carved her place in his heart. He'd made himself her protector, her champion and her knight, keeping her safe. He'd completely adored the little girl and would have done anything for her. Even then, when she was only ten and he fifteen, she'd been so much more than a little sister.

When his feelings for Giselle began to change

and grow into something else, instead of fighting it, he had chosen to tread carefully and listen a little more to his head than his heart. On the night of her fifteenth birthday, he'd sensed a change in her, one that made his heart sing. But she was still young and he couldn't be sure. He hadn't been sure of much of anything his emotions were so conflicted.

Seeing her on stage as Odette changed everything, and he knew he could no longer deny his feelings. He saw into her heart that night, just as she glimpsed into his own on Christmas morning. Nothing was the same after that.

Gilles' love for Giselle soon merged to an aching need, a desire that burned from the inside out, and he was powerless to stop it. He had worked so hard to leave her innocence intact. But on graduation night, his heart told him it was time.

So he kissed her. After months of surviving on her touch alone, he released his pent-up longing and lost himself in her kiss, and oh, how magnificent the moment! He'd never in his life experienced anything so amazing. He had dated girls here and there through the years, not because he really wanted to be with them, but because it was expected. But during a few of those times all he could think of was Giselle. The few times he did kiss a girl goodnight, in his head and heart he was kissing Giselle. When she was still so young and he had crossed over into adulthood, thoughts of her bothered him so much, he sometimes worried that there was something wrong with him, so he relentlessly worked on keeping them in check. Sometimes he was successful, sometimes not.

Gilles always knew he would marry Giselle. There could be no one else for him. He'd planned to marry her on her eighteenth birthday. But his love for her had grown to such enormous proportions that, just like the changing of the tide, his plans changed with his parents' trip. Living together in that house completely alone for a whole week would have been too much, and he was sure God knew that as well.

So before God, he married her, knowing their vows would be accepted by the only One that mattered. When they married at the courthouse today, it had only been in answer to a technicality, for the right to give Giselle his name.

And now she was truly his.

They would not worry about their parents now. They would let them deal with their problems, because their problems had nothing to do with him and Giselle. If his mom and dad chose not to accept their marriage when they returned, then Gilles would take his wife and leave and build their life together regardless.

They would be together. That was all that mattered.

J. Adams

Chapter 15

Verona, Italy

Mere words could never do justice to Verona. Called the city of love, history was everywhere.

When Shakespeare made it the home of Romeo Montague and Juliet Capulet, it was for good reason: romance, drama and fatal family feuds have been there for centuries. I read about the city during the flight. To actually be seeing it was amazing.

The travel guide said from the third century BC, Verona was a Roman trade centre, but Shakespearean tragedy became a part of the city. The man who conquered Verona in 569 AD., was murdered by his wife three years later. After Mastino della Scala (aka Scaligeri) lost re-election in 1262, he claimed absolute control until he was murdered by rivals.

I'm couldn't imagine being around then, but I was happy to reap the benefits of Verona's ageless beauty. The monuments and relics that filled the city were from medieval and Renaissance periods, making it a historian or artists' dream. I was completely fascinated, from the moment we flew in. Even driving through the streets was incredible.

We finally turned on to a private cobbled drive. I had seen many beautiful homes, including my own. However, the small villa Gilles rented for us had an indescribable beauty all its own.

The peach and beige stucco home sat high on a mountainside with a panoramic view of the lake and surrounding countryside. Out back, there was a covered stone terrace built with wide arched doorways. On the terrace were tables and chairs, each one topped with a candle. Beyond the heated pool stood a large olive grove. Inside the house, the furniture was a mix of antique and modern design, leather and baroque. Every room had an elegant Italian style atmosphere and the details were beautiful. The house had four suites and the living room boasted a large fireplace with a great view of the lake. The dining area was spacious and the huge kitchen was equipped with modern appliances and granite counter tops.

Gilles laughed at my giddiness over the place. I was experiencing major jet lag, but that took a back seat to my excitement just being there. There were plenty of apartments we could have rented that were just as beautiful, but Gilles wanted us to be completely alone. We chose the biggest suite to sleep in because it had a large skylight over the bed. The white silk draped canopy over the king-size bed added to the romantic feel.

We unpacked and put our things away, then made a quick trip to the market for groceries. After putting everything up, we decided to take a nap and rest up for our visit to Juliet's house. Gilles knew I would have to see it before anything else. Lying beneath cotton sheets with a summer breeze drifting through the open window, we quickly fell asleep.

* * *

I have always loved the story of Romeo and Juliet, so I was beyond excited to see the house. Gilles and I were among hundreds that day who gazed up at the balcony where Juliet stood while Romeo declared his love. It didn't matter that Romeo and Juliet may have only been figments of Shakespeare's imagination. The love story was powerful, even though the ending was tragic.

Juliet's house was owned by the family dell Capello. The name sounded very similar to Capulet. The house dated from the 13th century and the family coat of arms still hung on the wall. The balcony wasn't added until the 20th century, but that didn't sway me from stepping out on it to gaze down into the crowd at Gilles—my own Romeo. I wasn't bold enough to call for him like most of the women were doing to their significant other, but I did blow him a kiss and he caught it in the air. He took a picture of me leaning over the balcony and said he wanted to frame it. Near the balcony was the Shakespeare passage: *But soft! What light through yonder window breaks? It is the east, and Juliet is the sun. It is my lady; O, it is my love.*

Out in the courtyard, there was a bronze sculpture of Juliet. Gilles and I laughed as we watched people rub her right breast for luck. I squealed with delight as we looked at the hundreds of love notes stuck on the wall in the entrance to the courtyard. They were all addressed to Romeo. Though I was grossed out a little by the chewed up gum attaching many of the notes to the wall, it was still romantic.

Opening my tote bag, I took out a small folded note and a foil sticker and stuck it to the wall.

"So," Gilles said, wrapping his arms around my waist, "you're writing him, too, huh?"

I smiled, nuzzling my nose against his cheek. "I've got a feeling my Romeo will get this today . . .

like probably before we leave." I look up at him, grinning at his arched brow.

"Hmmm, I'm sure he will."

Before we entered the museum, he snatched the note from the wall and slipped it into his back pocket. "My wife the romantic." He kissed my hand and drew me close to his side.

Inside the house, there were many things on display that dealt with Shakespeare's work, as well as the films based on Romeo and Juliet. There were lots of pictures, photos and costumes. All the ceramics and furniture were authentic to the period. The museum even displayed the bed from the Franco Zeffirelli movie! I loved the whole experience.

Standing in the courtyard for a few moments before we left, I wrapped my arms around Gilles' neck and drew his head down, pressing my mouth to his, allowing the passion I felt for him to seep through. His soft growl in response sent heat rolling through me. "Thank you for this," I said, drawing back and seeing the emotion in his eyes.

"You're welcome." He kissed me again, his

arms tightening around my waist. "I would do anything for you, Giselle."

"I know."

J. Adams

Chapter 16

Gilles

Gilles and Giselle found a quiet restaurant off the beaten path away from the tourist's area and had dinner.

"You are a beautiful couple," the middle-aged waiter said when he reached their table to take their order.

"*Grazie*," Gilles replied, squeezing Giselle's hand across the table, smiling at the blush that crept into her cheeks. He asked the man to take a picture of them with Giselle's camera and he was delighted to do it.

After dining on chicken fettuccine Alfredo, Caesar salad and tiramisu, they paid the check and thanked the waiter for his service. In no big hurry, they sat and talked for a little while before heading back to their place.

While his wife was in the bathroom, Gilles took off his clothes and got into bed. Remembering the note Giselle taped to the wall at Juliet's house, he reached down and fished it out of his jean pocket. Smiling, he read it as tears blurred his vision.

Dearest Romeo,

How do I love thee? I love you more than it is possible to imagine. There are no words for the breath and depth of my love, no way to describe how my heat pines for you and how my being longs for your touch when you are away from me. You are every breath I take. Your essence is life to me.

Oh, my dearest love, just looking at you

overwhelms me. Gazing at your beautiful face and body, then during the shadows of night, being entwined with that same body, and my mouth worshiped by the blessed, heated wonders and affections of your own, is a life-giving communion I wish to partake of forever and ever.

I desperately adore you, my dearest Gilles. You were my knight from the beginning, my champion and shelter against the raging storms that have burst upon my life. Let them rage on in their hellish fury, I no longer fear them. As long as my hand is clasp tightly in yours, I will always know heaven.

Gilles leaned back against the headboard as tears rolled down his face. It seemed his wife was gifted in more ways than one.

* * *

When I came out of the bathroom, Gilles pulled me into bed and just held me. I hadn't missed the emotion in his red eyes. Glancing over at the table,

I saw the note and held him tighter.

"Thank you," he finally said. "Thank you for being my Juliet." Then he kissed me and there were no more words.

* * *

We spent the following day touring the different churches in Verona and we bought a few souvenirs. That evening we went to an opera, *IL Trovatore* by Giuseppe Verdi at the Arena Di Verona. Because there were three separate intertwining subplots, the story was kind of confusing, but I loved the music and the voices of the performers.

We spent the next two days touring Venice. There was a neat little shop along the canal that sold naturally scented handmade soaps and I bought several bars. In another shop I purchased a small crystal gondola, a carnival mask to hang on our bedroom wall, a couple Venice totes, and some souvenir t-shirts. Stopping in a quaint little shoe shop was an obsessive necessity and I purchased two pairs of Italian leather sandals. Gilles just grinned at me, shaking his head.

"It's a good thing you bought the totes. We made need a few more before the day is over."

I laughed. "I promise I'm done for today." He quirked a brow and I added, "Maybe."

We visited St. Marks Basilica and the other churches of Venice, cruised through the Grand Canal in a water boat during the day, and enjoyed a leisurely romantic ride in a gondola at night.

After Venice, we spent a day in Milan, shopping in malls and outlets. I found some great outfits, and so did Gilles. We purchased an extra, very large suitcase to take it all back in. I got a pair of shoes for Tanya. We bought some nice dress shirts and silk ties for Dad, and out of courtesy, we purchased a designer dress and purse for Gina, though neither of us felt like giving her anything. I wondered if she would even accept it, especially after we broke the news of our marriage.

* * *

The last two days were spent at the villa. We took walks through the olive grove and around the grounds. We swam in the pool, had a picnic out on the back lawn, snapped pictures of one another, and dined by candlelight out on the terrace. We savoured and made the most of every moment together.

On our final day, it rained and I was a little tired, so we just lay in bed and talked. Neither of us was looking forward to leaving, but it was time to go back and start our life. I just needed to keep my newfound courage intact. I only hoped that Dad and Gina were able to settle things between them. We did call him right after we'd landed in Verona to let him know we made it safely, and he said not to worry about them. He was planning to take Gina for a short getaway when we returned.

I adjusted my head on Gilles' chest. "Did your mom ever tell you how she met your dad?"

"No, but Dad did. He also told me how your parents met. Dad actually introduced them."

"Really?"

"Yeah. Dad said he and Mom met when she and your mom were vacationing in Italy. They'd treated themselves to a college graduation trip." He paused and we took a minute to ponder the irony. "Dad was born and raised in Rome. They met at a museum. Dad said he had a friend visiting from Wales. The four went out together and that was it. Mom and Dad got married and your parents married a few years later."

"I guess I was so young, Mama didn't think about telling me the story."

"Probably because she thought she would have longer and there would be time."

"You're probably right."

I couldn't help wondering why Gina agreed to take me in if she felt Mama betrayed her. Thinking on it, I was now convinced that it had really been Dad who wanted me. This made me love him even more.

Gilles touched my face, seeming to read my

thoughts. "It doesn't matter. None of it does." He turned over and rose over me, his gaze filled with so much adoration, tears stung my eyes. "I love you, Mrs. de Francesco."

"And I love you, Mr. de Francesco."

"So, we will tell them when we get back, then?"

I nodded. "Yes, we'll tell them. I could never go back to hiding. You're my husband. I'm your wife. We love each other and that is all that matters."

"Nothing else matters," he murmured softly as he lowered himself against me, immediately devouring my lips as passion quickly swirled around us, filling the room.

I didn't worry about leaving our little world anymore. Because now that world would come home with us, keeping us captive wherever we were.

Chapter 17

I slept during most of the flight to Chicago, then half of the flight to Salt Lake. I apologized to Gilles for not being much company. I was wiped out from the trip and he understood.

"Thank you, Gilles," I said as we drove to Park City. "I know I've said it many times, but it was an awesome honeymoon."

He smiled, kissing my hand. "You're welcome. We'll have to go back sometime and tour all of Italy."

"That would be awesome." I gave him a slow

smile. "You'll have to use your Italian more often."

"Okay, I will, but only during certain times, and only with you."

"Sounds good to me." I sighed dramatically and he chuckled.

When we arrived home, no one was there. We took our things and put them in my room. There would be no more sleeping apart. If things didn't work out the way we hoped, we would quickly find a place of our own.

Gilles called Dad. Dad said he was in Salt Lake and would be back later on. We looked forward to his return so we could break the news. I hoped and prayed he would understand.

Dad had asked Gilles to run and check on things at the lot. He kissed me and said he would hurry. I told him to take his time and I would be fine until he got back. After he left, I unpacked our dirty laundry and tossed it into the basket. As I picked up the basket to take it down to the laundry room, nausea rolled through my stomach. Dropping the basket, I made a beeline to the bathroom and threw up. Flushing the toilet, I pushed the hair back from my face and went to sink to rinse. I stood holding on to the counter top and took in my reflection, my heart beating hard as realization dawned on me. My period was three weeks late. I hadn't even thought about it until that moment.

Pulling my hair up in a bun, I splashed some water on my face, took a deep breath, then grabbed my purse and made a quick trip to the store, hoping with everything in me that I wouldn't run into anyone I knew. The last thing I wanted or needed right now were questions, though the wedding rings would bring questions as well.

Along with the pregnancy test, I grabbed a couple of extra things—a six-pack of Sprite, a box of Ritz crackers. At the moment, I didn't think I could stomach much else.

Three weeks late! My period was three weeks late and I had completely spaced it. *What a scatterbrain.* I guess that's what being in love with

Gilles did to me. Literally!

As I stood in line to pay, a pretty middle-age woman standing in front of me turned around and smiled.

"You know, they say most people spend an average of five years just standing in lines. Grocery store lines, movie theatres, DMV, restaurants, bus stops, etc. I don't know about you, but I tend to believe it."

I smiled. "I think you're right."

"Well, at least we get to meet people while we're waiting for whatever." She grinned and I was blown away by how cute she was. Her skin was a rich cocoa shade, her hair short and curly, and her brown eyes were exotic and shaped like almonds. A couple of inches shorter than my height of five-foot-six, she had a curvy figure and wore a colorful tunic over white leggings. Her face bore only a hint of makeup and I had the strongest urge to reach out and touch the dimple in her chin. I couldn't help watching her as she paid for her groceries. As she grabbed her two reusable shopping totes, she smiled again and said, "You have a great day, okay?"

"Thank you, you, too." I watched her walk away, grateful for the small tender mercy of standing in line behind her. For those few moments, my mind had been freed from worrying over being seen by anyone.

By the time I made it back, I was feeling sick again. Closing my bathroom door, I quickly took the test and then placed it on the counter while I knelt by the toilet and threw up again, extremely grateful that the urge hadn't come while I was out.

Glimpsing the positive test result was a bittersweet moment. I felt like laughing and crying at the same time. But more than anything, I felt tired and lost, and I hoped Gilles would be back soon so I could share the news with him and not feel so alone.

I threw the test stick and the package in the garbage. After rinsing again, I went to lie down. So many thoughts tumbled through my head. Since we couldn't legally marry until a week ago, there would definitely be questions from Dad and Gina. But as long as Gilles was with me, I would be able to handle whatever came.

I drifted to sleep with that thought at the forefront of my mind.

Chapter 18

"Giselle, wake up!"

Gina's voice jolted me awake. I opened my eyes to find her standing by the bed looking down at me, the expression on her face prompting me to quickly sit up. "Yes?"

"Looks like you've been busy," she spat.

"What do you mean?" I was a little nauseated again and not up to one of her fits.

"I mean this." She brought her hand from behind her back, shoving the test stick in my face.

"Looks like you are just as much of a slut as your mother."

A quiet anger filling me, I slowly stood. "My mother was not a slut and neither am I." Though I kept my voice even, inside I was livid. "Why were you snooping around in my bathroom?"

"It's my house, I can look anywhere I want."

"This is my room."

"No, it isn't. It never was. I never wanted you here, and I definitely will not be supporting an unwed mother."

I held up my hand. "I am married now." Her eyes widened and I continued on, wishing I could have told her under different circumstances. "Gilles is my husband."

"You're lying! He would never marry you!"

"He loves me. We've loved each other for a long time."

"You seduced my son, you whore! Get out of

my house!"

Take a deep breath and count to ten. "I will gladly leave when Gilles gets back."

"You will leave now. And we will have this sham of a marriage annulled."

Too emotionally and physically exhausted to argue, I grabbed my purse and keys. "I'll wait outside for Gilles."

"You just do that. You will never step foot in this house again." I left the room and she followed behind me, ranting on. "We gave you everything and this is the thanks we get? You sleeping with our son and tricking him into marrying you! You've probably been working on him for years, a child whore tempting him."

I didn't say anything or acknowledge her. And I definitely wasn't about to let her see me cry. On and on she ranted, saying things about Gilles and me that were so lewd I was shocked to hear them come out of her mouth. Her voice rose as I walked down the stairs.

She wanted to make sure I heard every sickening word. Before I reached the door, Gilles walked in followed by Dad. I went into my husband's arms."

"You cannot be married to this slut!"

"Gina!" Marco yelled.

"She's pregnant! She seduced our son and now she's pregnant!"

"Mother–and right now I use the title loosely– Giselle is my wife and she did not seduce me! We married because we love each other. We always have." He drew back a little, looking into my eyes, his expression full of love. "That's why you've been so tired. You're pregnant?"

I nodded. "I just took a test." I pulled him close again. "Are you okay with this?" I whispered in his ear. He drew back and nodded, caressing my face softly. The warmth in his eyes said everything.

"Are you listening to this, Marco?" Gina screeched. "He married her!"

"I know!"

"You . . . what? You've been in on it, haven't you? You knew."

"Not until a few minutes ago."

Gilles whispered to me, "I told him outside." His eyes begged me to understand. I tightened my arms around his waist, letting him know I did. He continued to whisper, "I only wish I had been here with you when you told *her*."

"He can't stay married to her," Gina went on.

Dad glared at her. "He can and he will."

"You would support this, wouldn't you? Because of Adesina, you would give Giselle anything, even condone her trapping our son into marriage."

"Giselle is officially my daughter now. Gilles is a big boy and they are two consenting adults. They're married and will stay married. Get over it!"

She looked at Gilles and me. "One day you will be sorry you did this. I hope you're miserable. I hope the day comes when you're as miserable as I am now."

"Get over yourself, Gina, and let them be!"

Her eyes narrowed as she glared back at Dad, her nostrils flaring angrily. Without another word, she grabbed her keys and purse off the entryway table and left, slamming the door behind her.

I turned to Dad. "Please don't be angry, Dad. We do love each other, more than anything."

He opened his arms and I stepped into them. "I know, honey. I know, and I'm not angry." He kissed my brow. "I've known you two were in love for a long time now." Sighing, he released me and walked into the family room, then wearily sat in the chair and we took a seat on the sofa. Gilles kept my hand in his, drawing me close.

"When did you know, Dad?" Gilles asked. "About us."

"Well, truthfully, I started realizing something was different in you on Giselle's fifteenth birthday. I had never seen you as miserable as you were when she went to that party with her friend. And I had never seen her so miserable to leave. But the day I truly knew was on Christmas when Giselle opened your present. I watched you watching her. When she pulled out that photo, I saw the way you were looking at each other and I knew. The emotion flowing between you two was so tangible, I could have wept." He smiled sadly. "I think your mother glimpsed something that morning, but she couldn't accept it and probably blocked it out, pretended it wasn't there. I think she has been pretending for a long while now." He looked at us intently. "Tell me about the pregnancy. You were only married last week."

"No, Dad," Gilles said, squeezing my hand. "We've actually been married since the day after graduation."

Dad's eyes narrowed. "How did–"

"We spoke our vows before God. A friend who is a minister officiated, as a favour to me. We exchanged rings and made our promises. In God's eyes, we were married. Then on our birthday we went to the courthouse and made it legal."

"You didn't have that long to wait. Why couldn't . . ." Dad paused and I could see the reason dawning on him. "I understand."

"Do you really, Dad?" I asked. "We need you to understand. You are all we have and your opinion is the only one that matters to us."

He reached for our hands. "I do understand, and I love you both."

"We love you too," I said, happy and grateful to have him on our side. I didn't know how things would play out with Gina, but as long as Dad–and God–were with us, we would be okay.

Chapter 19

After talking with Dad for a while, I left them to discuss business and went up to lie down for a bit. By the time I awakened, it was almost dinnertime. I quickly put the rest of our things away. The laundry basket was gone so I figured Gilles must have taken it down. I appreciated him being so thoughtful.

I found Gilles and Dad out on the deck grilling more steaks. Salad fixings were on the counter so I grabbed a bowl and prepared it. Taking some plates down from the cupboard, I placed them on a tray along with some silverware and glasses and took it outside. I set the table, blowing a kiss to Gilles before going back for the salad. I asked Dad if Gina had come back. He said no, that she was most likely venting to a friend about everything and probably wouldn't be home until late. I set a place for her anyway just in case.

While we enjoyed our dinner, Dad asked us about our plans. We told him we didn't know yet. We would most likely look for a place of our own because it would be too hard living there with Gina. It would be for the best. This saddened him, but he understood.

We excitedly discussed the baby. Dad said he was looking forward to being a grandpa. Gilles said our babies would be beautiful, and of course, I agreed.

After dinner, we sat in the family room for a while and told Dad about our trip. He said he missed Italy and would like to take Gina back one day. This reminded me of something that had been on my mind and I finally asked Dad about it.

"Why did you give me my trust money early?"

He smiled, his expression melancholy.

"Because I had a feeling that by the time you returned, you two would want to marry." His brow furrowed slightly. "Gina was livid when I told her what I did. I think deep down, she knew things were changing, but like I said before, she refused to see anything."

Gilles' eyes were sad. "Well, now she has no choice."

I had another question but was hesitant about asking it. "Dad?"

"What is it, honey?"

"Well . . . I know Gina might be back at any time, but I need to ask you something."

"Ask me anything."

I hesitated another moment, then pushed on. "The day we left, when Gina said those things, I noticed something pass between you two, and I know there is more to the story than you told us." When he looked away, I was certain he'd held back something. "Please tell me, Dad."

He stood and walked over to the window, staring out into the darkness. It was another full minute before he spoke.

"The day I walked into the Natural Gallery of Modern Art in Rome was the day my life completely changed. I happened to be standing behind two women who were studying a Van Gogh. One of them turned and smiled, and I had never in my life seen anything so beautiful. Then her friend turned. She was beautiful as well, but the first had captured my heart with just a smile. I introduced myself and shook hands with the women. Asking if I could join them, they said yes, and I walked with them through the rest of the gallery. We were shy, she and I, this woman who carried my heart in her pocket, so her friend did most of the talking. Her friend was a charmer, and I knew she would be perfect for my friend who was visiting from Wales.

"That night, we went out and the two hit it off. Soon after, I began to see more of her, my beautiful American girl. She and her friend were staying in Italy for a month.

"Sometimes she and I barely said anything to each other, but the words we did share were enough, and I was in love. After we had been seeing each other for two weeks, she unexpectedly told me she thought is was best if we were just friends. I begged her to tell me why, but she gave no explanation. I was hurt, but I accepted it. Then she started seeing my friend. And though my heart wasn't in it, I started seeing hers.

"The woman I loved soon went back to the States, but her friend stayed." Dad finally turned to look at me. He had tears in his eyes. "Part of my heart still ached for the woman I loved, but I knew it was hopeless, so I finally allowed myself to fall in love with her friend, and I married her."

I was so shocked I couldn't say anything. Gilles stood and went to Dad. "What are you saying?"

"Exactly what you think I'm saying, son." His eyes met mine again. "It wasn't until right before your father died that I found out what really happened. Hugh called me one day and confessed everything. It seemed he and Gina had a meeting of the minds and decided Adesina's fate and mine. Hugh had gone to your mother one day and told her I was secretly infatuated with Gina, but because I didn't want to hurt her, I kept my feelings for Gina to myself. Hugh also told her he really didn't stand a chance with Gina himself because she really cared for me. So Adesina stepped aside."

"Wow," I heard Gilles whisper.

I was mentally trying to work through it all. Dad really had been in love with Mama at one time, but Gina–and my own father–stepped in and changed everything. This only added a new layer to my dislike for Gina, as well as a dislike for the secret side of my father I never knew was there.

But while a part of me felt a little hurt and angry on Mama's behalf, mostly, I was grateful that things worked out the way they did. If they hadn't, I wouldn't have Gilles now. That was something I couldn't bear to think about.

"I believed you, Dad. We both did, about

nothing going on between you and Mama. She was a good woman and had a lot of integrity. She would never have betrayed a friend."

"No," Dad agreed. "She wouldn't. Her integrity was the thing I loved most about her."

"So now what?" Gilles asked.

Dad sighed, running a hand back through his hair. "I don't know. I still love your mother, but it hasn't been the same since that day in Seattle. A small part of what I felt for her died that day with her accusations. I've always been faithful, and I have tried to recapture what we had, but . . . it's gone. I see that now. And truthfully, I think her anger is partly out of guilt. I forgave her for her betrayal all those years before, just as I forgave Hugh. I just don't think she has ever forgiven herself, and sadly, Giselle, you are a reminder of what she did."

"Then why did she agree to take me after Mama died?"

"Because I wouldn't let her back out of the

agreement. I think she finally started to look at it as a way to make things up to your mother. But she could never fully accept you as part of the family. I am so sorry for that."

I rose and hugged him. "It doesn't matter. You more than made up for her lack of love. Thank you for that."

"You don't have to thank me, honey. You're easy to love." He released me and again looked out into the night. "She's been gone a long time."

Gina really had been gone a while. Maybe she was still venting. She left like that once before when she was angry about something, only she hadn't been as mad as she was this time.

A few minutes later, we saw the lights of a car pulling up.

"That must be her," Dad said. "I'll go and see if she will talk to me now."

Watching him hurry from the room, we sat down again and I rested my head on Gilles' shoulder.

"Tired?" he asked, caressing my arm.

"A little. You would think that after two naps I wouldn't be."

"It's probably the pregnancy. Not to mention everything else today."

"Yeah. I can't help wishing I could talk to Mama about things. I miss her so much right now."

"I know, babe." He held me close.

"I hope Gina will come to accept our marriage, because I really don't want to leave. I love this house. And what anyone else thinks about our marriage doesn't matter."

He kissed my cheek. "I feel the same. We moved here when I was ten. Before that, we lived in Rome. This place has always been home to me."

"Me too. More so than Seattle."

Dad finally came back. At the sights of the tears streaming down his face, we jumped up.

"What is it, Dad?" Gilles asked. "Is it Mom?"

Dad's shoulders shook and I reached for his hand.

"It was the police. There was an accident. Your mom . . . she ran into a semi. She was swerving to miss a deer and . . . she's gone."

I couldn't believe it! I just couldn't. We held him as sobs wracked his body and cried with him. Dad cried for his wife, Gilles for his mother.

And I cried for the loss of what could have been.

Chapter 20

Three days later, we held a small graveside service for Gina.

Mark Twain said, "The fear of death follows from the fear of life. A man who lives fully is prepared to die at any time." Somehow that seemed to fit Gina. Estranged from her mother for years, the bridge between the two women had been burned to oblivion and her mother wouldn't even make the trip for her own daughter's funeral. Dad said he never knew what happened between Gina and her mother, but Gina had never been a forgiving person.

Dad's sister sent a large flower arrangement. He said she never liked Gina.

During all the time the de Francescos lived in Park City, Gina made very few friends, but the ones she did have were in attendance, along with Dad's business acquaintances who were there to support him. It was a beautiful day. The sun was bright and the clear sky was a brilliant shade of blue. It was the kind of day Gina would have appreciated.

I sat between Gilles and Dad with my hands tucked in theirs, silently offering comfort. Though I had lived with the de Francescos since I was ten, their pain was far greater than mine. They lost a wife and mother. My loss didn't really have a name. Even still, the house felt emptier with Gina's absence.

The Mormon bishop officiating over the service was a long-time acquaintance of Dad's and had graciously agreed to do it. His words over the grave concerning Gina were vague, leading me to wonder if he knew her at all. Or maybe he did but couldn't come up with much to say that was positive about her character. Still, his spiritual comments were uplifting and rang of much truth.

After the final internment prayer, we stood and accepted handshakes and a few hugs. There were several raised brows from people who noticed Gilles' and my wedding rings, but only one person said anything. Tanya gave me a tense smile and hugged me, whispering, "So the secrets have finally come to light. Call me." Drawing forth a smile, I nodded, looking forward to, and dreading, the conversation. I hoped her friendship was unconditional.

After we arrived home, people came and went throughout the day, bearing food and kind words. Glancing at the full counter top, we wouldn't have to cook for a few days.

* * *

"How are you, Dad?"

The two of us sat on the wicker sofa out on the deck. My arm was draped around him, my head resting against his shoulder.

"I don't know," he answered, kissing my forehead. "I think I'm just numb right now." He gazed out into the distance. The sky was still the same brilliant blue, a contradiction to the events of the day. "I feel some guilt, regret."

"If you could go back, what would you change? *Would* you change anything?"

"I've given that some thought through the years. Frankly, I don't know if I would. To change one thing would be to change everything, including the things I *wouldn't* want changed." He hugged me close. "Like having you with us. I wouldn't trade the happiness you've given me for anything. And the happiness you have given to Gilles. I could never wish that away."

"But if I hadn't come . . . if Gilles and I hadn't . . ."

"No, Giselle. We can't do that. We won't do the what ifs. I wouldn't change a thing."

I believed him. He would never lie because he

wasn't made that way. In that, he was like Mama.

"I love you, Dad."

"I love you too."

We sat quietly for a while, tending our own thoughts. Gilles was out doing an estimate for someone who wanted some work done on their car, so the time was mine and Dad's. I don't know what I would have done without his influence in my life. He had no idea how great a man he was. I truly thought of him as my father. And now that I was married to his son, he really was.

"Are you really okay with our marriage?"

"I am more than okay, Giselle. I can't imagine a better woman for my son." His embrace tightened. "Don't ever doubt it."

* * *

As the days and weeks passed, healing slowly descended on the house and life went on. Dad stayed busy with the business. When he was home, he was contemplative, often sitting alone on the deck or in his office. That he was lonely was obvious. I think he'd been lonely for a long time, even when Gina was there, but at least she had been there. Now it was a different kind of loneliness. Still, we always tried to be there for him.

As for Gilles and I, some people were more understanding of our marriage than others, but it didn't matter. We were living our life for us. After my long conversation with Tanya, things finally clicked into place and all her questions about me were answered. And she understood. She truly understood.

By the end of September, I was almost sixteen weeks along and could feel little flutters of movement. It was an amazing experience. I had gone to see a midwife in Salt Lake three weeks before, but her husband got a new job out of state and she'd had to move quickly. She referred me to another midwife who lived right there in Park city. The woman moved there from California six months before, leaving many sad mothers whose babies she had delivered over the years. I was told she had twenty years of experience behind her and she would do a great job taking care of me. I made an appointment with her a few days before and would be going to see her that afternoon. Gilles planned to go with me, wanting to be involved in every aspect of my pregnancy. When I first told him I wanted to have the baby at home, I thought he would have concerns and worries, but he didn't. He said he would support me in whatever I wanted to do. I loved him so much for that.

J. Adams

Chapter 21

Grace Waters gave me the directions to her home and we found it easily. After developing such a great report with my previous midwife, I was a little anxious meeting Grace and was glad to have Gilles with me.

Grace lived in a small two-story house on Deer Valley Drive, one of Park City's main roads. The home had beige siding and green trim. The short sidewalk was lined with late blooming flowers.

When we parked, I thanked Gilles for coming

and he assured me he wouldn't want to be anywhere else. Sensing my anxiousness, he squeezed my hand as we walked to the door and gave me a quick kiss. There was a small "Come In" sign hanging above the doorbell. We opened the door and walked into a beautiful hardwood entryway. The walls were lined with framed prints of Anne Geddes artwork. I had always loved her stylized depictions of babies and motherhood. There were various photos of babies dressed as fairies, flowers and small animals.

"Cute," Gilles said softly.

"I know. I would love to order some of these for the baby's nursery."

"I can't think of a better thing to use my old room for."

"It will definitely be convenient having it just across the hall, and it will be easier to hear the baby."

"Good thing we redecorated your room last year. All that purple and peach would have driven me crazy now."

I chuckled, poking him. "I thought you liked the colors."

"When you were younger. If I had known then that it would be *our* room one day, I might have pushed for another color."

"I'm glad you like the earth tones I picked. I think I subconsciously picked those colors because of you."

Wrapping his arms around me, he caressed my small, rounded stomach, kissing me warmly. "It's nice to know we're so connected." His smile faded slightly. "Mom liked the purple. She was all about explosive colors."

He said nothing more and I held him close. The moments of grief were sporadic, and though the pain had eased up some, the scar would always be there.

A voice called from upstairs, "You're welcome to wait in the living room and I'll be right down."

"Thank you," I answered, wondering why the

voice sounded familiar.

We sat on the dark green floral sofa, which was situated near a gas fireplace. I glanced up at the collection of porcelain birds on the mantel. The red cardinal caught my eye because it stood out from the muted colors of the others. Its shiny coat shimmered in the sunlight streaming through the shuttered window.

When Grace entered, I couldn't have stopped the grin from spreading across my face if I tried. I could never forget the woman I met at the grocery store because she made such an impression.

She laughed. "I know you, beautiful lady!"

"And I know you! I can't believe it, Gilles. This is the woman I mentioned meeting at the store that day."

"It's good to meet you, Grace," Gilles said, shaking her hand.

"It's a pleasure to meet you, too, and I'm so glad to officially meet you, Giselle. You won't believe it, but I've thought a lot about you over the weeks.

Don't ask me why. I guess now I know."

"I've thought about you too."

She smiled. "Come on across the hall."

We followed Grace to a small examining room. It was bright and colorful with silk flowers and greenery covering the long high shelves that lined each wall. I would think they probably required a lot of dusting, but the air purifier in the corner most likely cut that chore down.

After answering some questions, she tested a urine sample and took my blood pressure. Then listened to the baby's heart. She measured my stomach and said the growth was on schedule.

"Tell me about yourself, Giselle. How long have you two been married and how did you meet?"

Gilles' eyes met mine, his gaze one of love and support. For reasons I couldn't explain, I wanted to share everything with this woman, so with Gilles' help, I did. We shared how we met as kids and became best friends when his family took me in after my mother's death. I told her about Mama and the amazing woman she was. Gilles told Grace about slowly falling in love with me. I opened up about our secret marriage, and finally, Gilles told her about losing his mother. Grace said ours was the most wonderful love story she'd ever heard. She was sorry to hear about Gina, but she was happy for our marriage. It was nice being able to share it freely and not be judged.

Grace finished her examination. "Everything looks great," she said. "Now Sarah told me you've decided on a water birth. Is that right?"

"Yes, I've read a lot about it and want to try it."

"Oh, I promise you will love it. It's a peaceful way to ease the baby into the world and the water is a natural pain reliever. Nature's epidural, we call it." She smiled at Gilles. "And you will be helping her the whole way, right?"

"Definitely."

"That's what I like to hear."

"Grace, what brought you to Park City?" I

asked.

"Well, it's sort of a long story. My life in many ways is like one of those tragic novels, but not irreversibly tragic because I'm still here." She looked at her watch. "You two in a hurry?"

"No," Gilles answered. He looked at me and I smiled.

"We've got time," I told her.

"All right, let's go into the kitchen. I've got some lemonade and pound cake. If you're going to listen to my story, the least I can do is feed you."

Gilles squeezed my hand and grinned, and I could tell he was just as taken with Grace as I was.

* * *

"Wow!" Gilles said for the fifth time as we drove home and I mentally echoed the sentiment. Grace's life story really did mirror one of those novels that became made for TV movies.

Grace was raised in Los Angeles with twin

brothers. Two years younger than her brothers, they always watched out for her and the three were very close. At eighteen, Grace married Melvin Hinds, one of her brothers' friends. She loved him and had high hopes for a wonderful life together, and for the first year, things were great.

Then her brothers Andrew and Peter enlisted in the Marines, completely unaware of how vulnerable they left their sister. A few months after they left, Melvin began abusing Grace. Never one to take things lying down, Grace fought back, but each time she did, the beatings intensified. So she stopped fighting.

A year after they married, Grace gave birth to a little girl. She hoped that fatherhood would soften Melvin and things would get better, and for a year they did. Then he started drinking and things slowly returned to the way they were, only now she had a child to protect, too.

Melvin was a functioning drunk and worked during the day in sanitation. To others, he was one of the kindest guys you could ever meet, but behind closed doors he was another man entirely.

When little Amy turned two, Melvin began to abuse her. If she cried a lot, he would get mad and hit her. Grace didn't know until she started noticing bruises. Then came the fateful day that she walked in right when he'd picked Amy up and thrown her against the wall. When the child didn't move, he ran off, leaving Grace screaming and sobbing. By the time the paramedics got there, it was too late and the little girl died. There was an immediate warrant out for Melvin's arrest.

Grace was so deep in grief she could barely function. She moved back home with her parents for a while and slowly healed. She had a friend who was a midwife and began to apprentice under her. Two years later she became licensed and started her own practice.

The next year, Melvin came out of hiding and tracked Grace to her parents' home. At the time of his arrival, Grace's brothers were home on leave because their father had just passed away from diabetes. Neither of the men were married yet and both were more fiercely protective of their sister than before. When Melvin came over, Andrew and Peter were gone on a grocery store run for their mother.

Grace barely opened the door. Seeing who it was, she tried to close it, but he pushed it open. She yelled for her mother to run. He yanked Grace by the hair and started hitting her. He was a big guy and was able to fling her like a rag doll. It was then that her brothers entered and two shots were quickly fired. Melvin fell, dying instantly from one gunshot to the head, another to the heart. Both Andrew and Peter had fired their weapons.

Neither brother returned to the military. After serving some prison time (it had been ruled that two shots had been unnecessary) they started over again, married, and settled close to their mother. When Grace turned thirty, she married Doctor Sam Waters, a prominent physician who emotionally battered her and was a complete control freak. Less than a year later, before she could file for divorce (she was determined not to go through another abusive marriage) he was killed by a drunk driver.

Now the sole owner of a million dollar home and a sizable bank account, Grace continued her midwife practice. A year ago, she turned forty-four and decided she needed a change. After an extended vacation in Park City, she purchased her home, sold the one in LA, packed up everything, and moved. She has been happy living in Park City. Sadly, she was never able to have another child, but being a midwife soothed the hurt and she didn't think about it anymore.

* * *

"She's an amazing woman," I said later on that night.

"She is."

Gilles lay beside me, caressing my bare stomach. His hand was so large it almost covered my whole stomach. After putting in some dance time earlier, I was tired and had gone to bed early, but I still couldn't sleep. I couldn't stop thinking about all Grace shared with us.

"I have a feeling she and I are going to be great friends."

"I think so too."

"You're so agreeable tonight."

He smiled, rising over me. "I can't help it." He lightly pressed his mouth to mine. "That's what you do to me," he murmured.

"Okay then," I breathed as he took me in his arms.

Chapter 22

I slept in the next morning. When I awoke, Gilles was sitting next to me. He had already showered and was wearing clean jeans and a black t-shirt that hugged his sculpted arms and chest. His hair was still damp, a small lock falling against his forehead. He was utterly beautiful without even trying. The leather notebook he'd written in for years was lying on his lap and he was scribbling away. When I sighed, he looked at me, smiled and closed it.

"Good morning, beautiful," he said, leaning down to kiss me.

"Hey. Sorry I slept so long."

"Don't be sorry. You sleep as long as you need to. You're entitled. But now that you're awake, I have something to talk to you about."

"Okay, but can you wait a minute? My bladder is calling."

"I can do that," he said, chuckling as I hurried to the bathroom.

I quickly brushed my teeth before going back out. Slipping back into bed, I snuggled up to him. He smelled amazing, like Irish Spring soap and the Davidoff Cool Water cologne he always wore. I inhaled as he held me close.

"So Dad and I were talking this morning about a couple of things. I wanted to run them by you and find out how you felt."

"Okay."

"First, Dad offered to let me build my shop right on the dealership property. It would be a separate small building. That way, if one of his cars needed custom detailing, I would be right there. I would also hire another experienced guy to be there when I'm not, and a secretary. Since Dad's business will go to me one day, it makes sense. We don't know why we didn't think of it before. What do you think?"

"I think it sounds perfect!" His dream was finally coming true and I was excited for him.

"Are you sure?"

I kissed him. "Positive."

"All right, I'll let Dad know and we can get started. Now, about your studio. Dad and I were thinking that we should expand the garage I've been working out of and create a studio for you. You would be working from home, so to speak."

"Really? Dad would let me do that?" I couldn't believe it!

"Dad would give you the moon if he could, Giselle. So would I."

I laughed and hugged him tight. I would finally get my own studio!

"I take it that's a yes?"

"Yes! I would love it. I just can't believe it."

"Believe it. You're getting your studio and I'm getting my shop." He kissed me with a hint of passion. "I love you," he murmured.

"I love you."

With longing in his eyes–a look I knew well– he smiled at me, releasing me long enough to lock the door.

* * *

The construction on both businesses began immediately. I walked out frequently and watched Gilles with the other men as they worked on the studio. Watching Gilles, whether he was measuring pieces of lumber or putting up drywall, or even just standing talking with the men, always produced butterflies in my stomach. Somehow he would sense me near, even hear my sigh, and there would be no space between us.

Within three weeks, the studio was done. Gilles and I celebrated by having a picnic dinner on the freshly installed hardwood floor. Double the size of the former garage, there were now two big windows on either side of the entrance, and small square ones placed up high along the walls. Floor-to-ceiling mirrors covered one wall, a long barre extending the entire length. A small bathroom was built in one corner. Soft music came through the speakers of the built-in stereo system. There were large posters of Mikhail Baryshnikov, Margot Fonteyn and Rudolph Nureyev hanging on a far wall. It was a beautiful studio, more beautiful than I ever imagined.

Gilles stuck a disc in the player and helped me up, taking me in his arms. We danced slowly, my eyes closing at the feel of his lips against my brow. He was such a great dancer and was always the perfect partner because he was so versatile. He told me once that it was his Italian blood that had given him rhythm.

"Thank you for this. I appreciate you and Dad more than I can say."

"You deserve it. You're going to do well and your students will love you."

"I hope so. So far I have seven lined up. I'm so excited to begin."

"I'm excited for you."

"I'll teach until I can't anymore, then after the baby is born, I'll start again. It will only be three hours a week. Should be easy enough to handle."

"And I'll make sure I'm here in the evenings so you don't have to worry about the baby."

"If it's a girl, she will learn to dance early, and if it's a boy, I can see him working on cars when he's a toddler, or vice versa."

Gilles laughed. "Sounds like a plan."

When we finally went back into the house, I went to Dad's office and thanked him again.

"You're welcome," he said, hugging me. "Your

husband knew exactly what you'd like." His smile was slightly sad. "It's wonderful that he knows you so well."

"He loves me," I said simply. "And I love him madly."

"I know. And that love will see you through whatever comes in life."

J. Adams

Chapter 23

The following day, I was so nauseated, I couldn't even get up to get ready for my appointment with Grace, so she came to me instead.

I looked a sight when she entered the room, but I was too sick to care. I had thought I was over the morning sickness, but Grace assured me this was normal. I groaned into the pillow, the slightest movement making me feel seasick.

"I'm afraid this happens with a lot of mothers, sweet girl. You can feel great for weeks, then suddenly feel terrible for a day or two. I brought a box of ginger tea for you. It should help. If it's all right, I'll go make you a cup."

I smiled. She called me 'sweet girl.' It was what Mama always called me. "Thank you, Grace."

"You're welcome. Now Gilles, you just point me toward the kitchen and I'll take care of that while you take care of your wife."

"Okay, just turn right at the bottom of the stairs and keep going. It's just past the formal dining room."

"Got it. Be right back."

"Gilles, I love her," I said after Grace left the room.

"I know. So do I. Nothing against your old midwife, but Grace is amazing."

"She is. She kind of reminds me of Mama in a way."

"I can see it."

Turning on my back and swallowing against a

strong wave of sickness, I squeezed Gilles' hand. "I'm sorry. I don't want to keep you from your work. You should go and check on the progress of your shop."

"No, I should be here with you. The shop is almost done, probably by the end of next week."

"I'm so excited for you."

"So am I. The only drawback is being farther away from you."

"Well, on the days that I'm feeling okay, I can come by and visit you for a bit."

"That would be awesome."

The familiar sound of Dad's voice and Grace's laughter carried down the hallway.

"Your father was shocked to come home and find a strange woman in his kitchen rifling through the cupboards."

"Not shocked," Dad countered, "just pleasantly surprised."

"He says that now," Grace teased and Dad

made a face.

Gilles laughed. "I see you've met Grace, Dad."

"I have." He smiled. "It's a pleasure, Grace."

"Same here." She placed the cup of ginger tea on the nightstand, along with a piece of wheat toast. "You think you can sit up and take in a little of this?"

Attempting to ignore the queasiness produced by moving, I sat up a little and leaned back against the headboard. Gilles handed me the tea and I took a sip, then two more, the slightly spicy liquid immediately beginning to calm my stomach.

"Better?" Graced asked.

"Yes." Then to Gilles, I said, "We should get a supply of this stuff."

"I'll grab some more today."

I took a bite of the toast while Grace checked my pulse. Dad again told Grace he was glad to meet her and excused himself. Gilles walked out with him, saying he would only be gone a moment.

After Grace listened to the baby's heart, I felt okay enough to get up and give her a urine sample. She talked with me for a few minutes and said everything looked good.

"So have you decided where you want to have your baby? I have a birthing suite in my home or I can bring a portable tub and you can have it here. Whatever you prefer is fine."

"I think I'd like to have it here."

"Sounds good. I have a list of birthing supplies you will need. If you want, I can order everything for you and have it delivered here, or if you would prefer to do it, that's fine, too. We still have plenty of time."

"If it's not too much trouble, I'll let you do it. Just let us know the total and we'll write you a check."

"Okay." She packed up her bag. "Now drink a cup of tea every few hours or so until you feel better. And try to eat some small meals, and drink plenty of water. We don't want you dehydrated or weak from not eating, though sometimes the latter can't be helped.

But take in what you can."

"I will." I watched her scribble some things down on a notepad. "Are you taking care of many mothers right now?"

"At the moment I have four others. Two are due in November, one in January and one in February. Things are slower here, but I don't mind. It just means I have more time to take care of you." Her words brought tears to my eyes. It had been a long time since I'd had real motherly care. It felt nice. She noticed my tears before I could dry them. "What's wrong, baby?"

"Nothing," I said, smiling. "I just appreciate you a lot. Thank you."

The look in her eyes said she understood. "I'm glad to be here."

* * *

After Grace left, I managed to get up and shower. Afterward, I made the bed and straightened the room a bit before lying back down and quickly falling asleep. When I woke up, Gilles was curved around me, sleeping. Taking in his smooth features, I touched his face, surprised to find it hot. In fact, his whole body was warm. He slowly opened his eyes and smiled.

"Gilles, you have a fever. Are you feeling sick?"

"I think I've caught something. The fatigue just hit me all of a sudden, so I figured I would just nap with you for a bit."

I sat up and looked at the clock. "A bit? Gilles, it's almost three. You slept for quite a while, and you're not even pregnant."

"Thank goodness for that." He grinned.

"Well, I'm feeling better, but maybe you should get in bed."

"I'm okay, Giselle, just a little headache, but I'll take some Tylenol and be fine."

"Okay, I'll grab some for you, then you can lie here for a bit until you feel a little better."

"Yes, dear."

"You!" I kissed his brow and went to grab some Tylenol from the bathroom. He took it and lay back down. "I'll go down and fix something for dinner."

"Okay. Be down in a few."

I kissed him again, hoping the fever would go away soon.

Chapter 24

Gilles felt better when he came down for dinner. I had thrown together a quick chicken scampi dish that didn't taste half bad. Gilles ate a good helping–not as much as he usually did–but he and Dad left very little in the pan. I didn't try to eat too much, just a few bites, along with another cup of ginger tea.

Afterward, we sat around the table looking at paint swatches for the nursery. Since we wouldn't know if it was a boy or a girl until the birth, we were looking through neutral colors. After twenty minutes of deliberating, we decided on green and beige–to be specific, mint and suede. We joked about all the different shades of green and their exotic names. Then I listened to Dad's long-winded oratory on how different men and women were. "Mars and Venus," he kept saying. But men wouldn't want us women any other way. It was the way of the universe.

Gilles said that if he was feeling up to it tomorrow, he would take me shopping for baby things. I asked him if he planned to go to his shop tomorrow. He said it could wait.

"I don't want to keep you from doing what you need to do," I told him as we got ready for bed.

"You're not. This is more important to me."

"If you're sure."

"I am."

I went to the bathroom once more, hoping I could make it through half the night without having to get up again. When I came back out, Gilles was already kneeling by the bed waiting for me. The day we married, we began praying together and we never missed a night. It was something that was now as natural to us as breathing, and we were closer because of it.

I was so tired, I fell asleep almost as soon as my head hit the pillow, but not before telling Gilles I loved him. He whispered he loved me too.

* * *

"Gilles, are you all right?"

It was the middle of the night and he had gotten up to take more Tylenol.

"Just a little achy. I think I've caught a bug. Hopefully it's just one of those twenty-four hour ones. I just don't want to get you sick."

I held him close. He was warm, but not like before. "If I'm going to catch it, nothing can stop it. We share the same germs now, remember?"

"Yes, ma'am." I could hear laughter in his voice. "Sorry to wake you."

"It's okay. I have to use the bathroom anyway.

Your child seems to enjoy these midnight trampoline jumps on my bladder."

He chuckled. "I will have to talk to him or her about it when he or she makes an appearance."

"I'd appreciate that," I said, getting up, grateful for the radiant-heated floors in our home. It made walking across the hardwood in the wintertime much nicer.

When I returned to bed, Gilles was lying on his back with his hands behind his head. The only light was from the half-moon spilling through the window. Gilles pulled me into his arms and I rested my head against his chest. The room was chilly, but he was my own private furnace. Even when he wasn't sick, he was always warm. He said his mom told him it was the same with his dad.

They were so much alike, he and Dad. They both possessed so much love inside. Gilles had me to pour his love upon and Dad had us. Even when Gina was alive, she refused to accept Dad's love. She refused what was available to her in abundance. I still felt sorry for her sometimes because of what she missed out on, not only now, but while she lived. And that was just it. She never lived.

I never wanted to be like that. I wanted to take every day and make the most of them, to live my best life in every single minute.

Just like Grace.

For a woman who had lost so much, Grace was truly a happy person possessing an upbeat soul and iron will that would let nothing get her down. I was sure she had her moments, even though she never said so. But she was an inspiration to me and I loved everything about her.

"What are you thinking about, beautiful?" Gilles' voice was soft and soothing in the silence.

"I was thinking about Grace. And Gina."

"Two women at opposite ends of the spectrum."

"I know." I caressed his chest, knowing what he was about to say.

"I miss her."

"Me too. Even though we weren't close, I do miss her. I don't understand why with the way things were between us."

He kissed my temple. "Because you have a kind and giving heart. You can't help but feel compassion toward her, regardless of how she treated you. Sometimes a part of me still feels sad about the way she was, but the anger is gone. It is never good to hold on to bitterness. I've learned that from you."

"And I have learned how to be brave from you."

"I guess that's why we're so perfect together, because we learn from each other."

I silently agreed. I didn't know where I would be without Gilles. He was my rock. Deep inside, I believed there was someone for everyone, and that Gilles and I were made for each other.

"Do you think she is happy for us now, Gilles?"

"I don't know." He brushed his lips against my brow. "I hope so."

"Me too."

I finally fell asleep, lulled by the gentle movement of our child.

J. Adams

Chapter 25

Gilles was tired a lot in the week that followed and he hardly ate anything. I braced myself to catch whatever he had, but I continued to feel fine, other than the moments of pregnancy nausea.

One day I woke to fine him gone. He'd left a note saying he had gone to check on things at the shop and I was relieved that he was feeling better. I got up, took a shower and dressed. Twenty minutes later, Gilles was back and again said he didn't feel well.

I sat on the bed next to him. He lay on his side

with a hand wrapped around mine. "What can I do?" I asked him, hating to see him so weak. He also looked like he had lost a little weight.

"Nothing, babe. I'll be okay." He scooted over and I lay down, curling into him. "I'll be fine, okay? Just lay here with me for a bit."

But he didn't get better, even after napping all day. That night he woke up again in pain.

"Gilles, we need to get you in to see the doctor. You're not getting any better and I'm going out of my mind worrying about you."

"I know, baby . . . I'll go tomorrow . . ."

I sat up in the dark. "You don't sound good. What is it?"

"Having a . . . hard time breathing."

Jumping up, I turned on the light.

Gilles' forehead was covered with sweat and his breathing was shallow, like he couldn't catch a breath. Grabbing the phone, I quickly dialed 911 and requested an ambulance. After answering a series of questions, I was told help was on the way.

"I'll be right back, Gilles. I'm going to get Dad. Paramedics are coming."

His grip tightened on my hand. "Stay," he rasped. "Please."

By now, tears were streaming down my face. "Okay, I'm here. I'm right here." I grabbed my cell from the desk and returned to his side and he quickly took my hand again. I dialed the house number. After the third ring, Dad picked up.

"Dad, it's Gilles. Something is wrong. He can hardly breathe. I called for an ambulance."

"I'm coming, honey."

A few seconds later, Dad rushed into the room. Since Gilles was too weak to even sit up, Dad helped me get a t-shirt and pants on him. I slipped a pair of socks on his feet. Through it all, I cried, terrified of losing my husband. In all the time I'd known him, Gilles had never been sick. He had always been completely healthy.

I prayed as I got dressed, prayed the doctors would be able to take care of whatever it was and he would be well again. I prayed without ceasing.

Gilles said he needed me. I reached for his hand and he held mine close to his heart, never letting go. His blue eyes met mine and he tried to smile, but they had lost some of their luster and that frightened me too. More tears trickled down my cheeks.

"Don't cry, Giselle. It'll be okay."

Dad went to get dressed and turn on the porch light. When he returned, he sat down, putting an arm around me.

"He will be all right," he said over and over. It was almost like a chant and I latched on.

And I prayed.

Chapter 26

Leukemia is such a solitary word, and certainly one I never imagined hearing in the same sentence as Gilles' name. My mind zoned in and out as we listened to the doctor's professional yet gentle rundown.

"The blood work suggests acute myelogenous leukemia."

Cancer.

"When you have leukemia, the bone marrow starts to make a lot of abnormal white blood cells, called leukemia cells. They don't do the work of normal white blood cells, they grow faster than normal cells, and they don't stop growing when they should."

My husband has cancer.

"Over time, leukemia cells can crowd out the normal blood cells. This can lead to serious problems such as anemia, bleeding, and infections. Leukemia cells can also spread to the lymph nodes or other organs and cause swelling or pain."

I could lose him.

"Acute leukemia gets worse very fast and may make you feel sick right away."

Our child could lose his father.

"He doesn't have any of the typical risk factors–smoking, radiation exposure, exposure to chemicals. The cancer has been there for quite some time, the symptoms only showing up recently. Fatigue, body aches, headache blurred vision, trouble breathing."

This can't be happening.

"We need to do a bone marrow biopsy. After a conclusive test, we need to start chemotherapy and radiation. With induction therapy, we work on achieving remission by killing as many leukemia cells as possible and returning the blood counts to normal."

I can't lose him.

"His blood is so low, we'll need to do a transfusion after the biopsy. In a couple of days, he will be transferred to Huntsman to start aggressive treatments."

Through the entire explanation, my hand was in Gilles', my eyes locked with his. He was on oxygen and was breathing better, but in his eyes I could see that the prognosis had changed everything. In them I glimpsed fear, I could see the little boy he once was. I also saw strength, hope, courage, and above all, I saw love, his desperate and hopeless love for me. When he smiled, I knew the same love was mirrored in my eyes. He would make it through this. I would stay by his side and he would make it. His determined look pushed my earlier thoughts of despair away. His gaze was one that said, *'You are my wife, you're carrying my child, and I will not leave my family.'*

The nurse finally came in to give him something for the pain and within minutes, he was asleep. I sat and watched him. Dad sat next to me, keeping my free hand in his, needing the contact as much as I did.

Grace called me on my cell, just checking up on me to see how I was feeling and if I needed anything. She said she was at the hospital with a birth mother who went into labor too early to chance delivering it at home. Everything had gone well with the delivery and Grace was about to head home. I told her about Gilles. Within a minute she was there and I was wrapped in her motherly embrace. I felt Dad's familiar caress on my hair and Grace included him in her embrace. I felt a quiet sob roll through him, unable to comprehend how hard this must be for him too. He had already lost a wife, now he was in danger of losing a son, my husband.

Grace drew back and pressed a hand to my

cheek. "Have you eaten?" I shook my head. "I'll run down to the cafeteria and get you something."

"You mind if I come along?" Dad asked.

"Not at all."

"Will you be okay, honey?" he asked me.

"I'll be fine. You go ahead. And thank you."

Grace smiled, then she and Dad left.

I sat next to the bed, taking Gilles' hand in mine again, a smile creeping to my lips. "I wish you could have seen what I just saw, Gilles. The way Dad's eyes lit up when Grace came in was priceless. They're getting along well. Wouldn't it be great if . . . well, we'll see."

Falling quiet, I turned his hand over in mine, palm side up, then back again, taking in the map of veins beneath his skin. If ever there was a pair of hands with the perfect blend of beauty and masculinity, it's his, possessing equal amounts of strength and gentleness.

A deep sigh escaped me as I thought of the warm touch of those hands in the night. Gazing up at his sleeping face, love overwhelmed me and my heart ached. Pressing my face against his side, I sobbed into the sheet, hurting in part for myself, but mostly for Gilles, because of what he would be facing. Witnessing what Mama went through, I knew the treatments were no picnic and he would suffer. I watched Mama go through it and then I lost her. I can't lose Gilles.

Some people may say Gilles and I were being punished for marrying. Some may say we weren't supposed to be together and this was our reward. I could allow myself to believe Gina's final ill wish for us had come to past.

I could allow myself to wallow in those kinds of thoughts. But I wouldn't.

"Please, God," I whispered into the damp sheet, "please don't let me lose him. Please don't take him away from me."

"Don't cry, Giselle," came Gilles' raspy voice. I sat up and met his anguished eyes, tears trailing down his face. "Come here, baby."

He opened his arms and I moved into them. He held me and we cried together, then he voiced what his eyes said earlier. That he loved me more than anything and he would not leave me. He would fight this with everything in him, for our future together.

Then we prayed together, knowing that our future, with all its uncertainties, was in God's hands.

* * *

By the time Dad and Grace returned, Gilles was asleep again. They brought me a sandwich and a salad, which I quietly ate by Gilles' side. After I finished, I took his hand in mine again. Dad and Grace stood by the window, talking quietly. She held one of his hands while he wiped his eyes with the other and I was grateful for her presence, grateful that she could be there to comfort him.

Gilles was soon taken down for the bone

marrow biopsy. Since the recliner I sat in doubled as a bed, I planned to stay the night. There was no way I could leave. I wouldn't.

Chapter 27

Two days later, Gilles was transferred to the Huntsman Cancer Institute in Salt Lake City, one of the best cancer facilities in the nation.

The first week of treatments was gruesome and the second was no better. Gilles was so out of it most of the time, I was surprised he knew I was there, but he always did. He hated me seeing him so weak, especially during the times that he was so sick, he couldn't even keep liquid down. The doctor would increase the nausea medication and he'd sleep for a while, but when he woke up, it would begin again.

During the third week, he had a few good moments. He also began to lose his hair that week. Sitting by his side, I knitted him some soft hats to keep his head warm.

Gilles' favorite thing to do was have me sit on the bed so he could rest his hand on my stomach and feel the flutters of the baby. Sometimes I would lay beside him and hold him, and no matter what, his hand was always on my stomach. I was in my twenty-third week and according to Grace, everything was going well. She did say she thought it was going to be a big baby, which explained why I felt huge already and was making bathroom runs every hour. I saw the inside of the hospital bathroom so often my mind had come up with redecorating ideas.

I always filled him in on what was going on at home when I was there, which wasn't much because I spent most of my waking minutes with him. I told him we put the Christmas tree up, but it wasn't the same without him. We even missed having Gina there delegating the decorating.

Grace was there and brought her own special joy with her presence. She and Dad had been spending a lot of time together and had grown close. Grace came to dinner twice a week and even helped with the cooking. She loved being there and I was sure Dad loved having her there just as much. They were planning to go out on their first official date that night.

"You'll have to talk to Dad when he gets home and ask him how it went."

"If I'm there when he gets back."

"Why wouldn't you be?"

"I might still be here."

Gilles sighed. "Giselle, you don't have to stay so late."

"I like being here until you go to sleep. Besides, I still have such a hard time sleeping without you, the only way I do is if I stay up late."

"But the drive home has to be getting hard, even if it is just every other night."

"I'll be fine."

"But you need more rest, for the baby."

"I said I'm fine." It had come out sharper than I meant it to. Lowering my head, I whispered, "I'm sorry." I couldn't tell him how afraid I still was. Afraid that one of these mornings I might come back to find him gone, having lost him in the night. I couldn't bear it. At the squeeze of his hand, I looked up.

"You know the leather notebook I've always written in?"

"Yes."

"I want you to read it." When I shook my head, he said, "Please read it. For me, okay?"

"Why, Gilles?"

"Because when you do, you will understand." He drew me closer, his voice softening. "When you do, you will know."

"Know what?"

"Read it for me, okay?"

"Okay."

* * *

On the day that marked his fourth week, Gilles wasn't feeling too well. I had gotten to know Dr. Peterson over the course of Gilles' treatments and trusted him implicitly. He said there was no sign of cancer in Gilles' blood and things were looking good. He would still be on the medicine for a while, but Dr. Peterson was amazed at how well he'd responded to the treatments. He said Gilles could probably go home the next day. Dad and I were elated by the news.

I kissed Gilles goodnight and settled myself in the recliner bed, looking forward to taking him home, longing to sleep beside him in our bed again. It had been so long since I'd fallen asleep with his arms around me. It was also great to know he would be with us for Thanksgiving

It seemed like I had only just shut my eyes when I was awakened by the nurse. They needed me to move. There was something wrong with Gilles.

I stood back out of the way, wringing my hands as they examined him. He wasn't moving. I could still hear the hiss of the oxygen, see the slight rise and fall of his chest, but he wasn't moving. Dr. Peterson asked me to step out into the hall while they worked on Gilles. Numb and in shock, I left the room.

A while later, Dr. Peterson exited Gilles' room and spoke a single sentence that swept my legs from under me.

"Gilles is in a coma."

Chapter 28

The days rolled by and I prayed.

* * *

I prayed.

* * *

I prayed.

* * *

I prayed.

* * *

And through the days of praying, I began to listen with my heart, and I learned some things.

Chapter 29

Two weeks later

Gilles was finally home.

The furnishings in our bedroom had been rearranged and now included a hospital bed near the window where my husband lay, unmoving. Dr. Peterson said coma patients lived on no one's time table. He still didn't know why it happened. There was no explanation. He said Gilles could wake up any day now, or he may never wake up. For this reason, I wanted him home where I could take care of him.

Hospice would visit once a day for a while. Then the visits would be cut back to three days a week. Dr. Peterson would also visit once a week. He lived in Park City, so he would stop by on his way home. The rest of the time, Dad and I would watch over him.

The sun was out, the warmth of its rays penetrating the windowpane, comfortably heating the area where Gilles lay. Sitting on the bed, I took his hand and pressed it against my lips then held his palm to my face. Leaning in, I gazed down at his hairless features. He'd not only lost his hair, but his brows and lashes as well. His weight was down a good twenty-five pounds and his muscles weren't as defined. Even still, he was the most beautiful thing in the world to me.

I pressed a kiss into his palm and another against his lips. Then, as was my routine, I talked to him, sharing my thoughts as if he were awake.

"I've learned some things over the past little while, Gilles. Some very important things that I know you will understand.

"First: I know there is a reason for everything, and everything we go through in this life is for a purpose. Not having you to lean on these past couple of weeks has taught me to be strong. Even when you were awake in the hospital going through your treatments, I was still leaning on you. I bet you didn't know that, did you? But now I have learned to lean on God more, which is really the way it should have been in the first place. Remember what I told you yesterday? About seeing Gina's friend Rhoda at the store and what she said to me? I think at another time, hearing the words, "You and Gilles brought this on yourselves because your marriage is wrong," would have broken me a little. But instead, her hurtful statement fell on deaf ears. I know our marriage is right, that you were made for me and I for you. No one will ever convince me otherwise. Like I said, there was a reason you came into my life.

"Second: I used to think that I wasn't good enough for you. You never did or said anything to make me feel that way, I just did. Maybe it was because of the opinions of others, I don't know, but I've learned a great lesson. Eleanor Roosevelt once said, "No one can make you feel inferior without your consent." Brilliant words, and there has never been a truer statement. If the opinions of others bring me down, it is because I allow them to. I know that now, and the only opinion that should matter is God's. I have engraved that in my heart now.

"Third: I can't let the world determine my worth. I think this is something I've always done, especially with Gina when she was here. I can't allow my value to be deemed by society. I watch so many people we know value unimportant things and try to conform to the masses instead of recognizing why we are really here. The world doesn't know me . . . but God does, and so do you. The world doesn't care what is inside me, or what I deal with daily. The world doesn't know my hopes, dreams, fears, or what touches me deep inside . . . but God does, and so do you. The world has no clue what is important to me, or you. It couldn't care less. But the world tries to dictate our importance. We can't let it.

"Fourth: I wouldn't wish this trial on anyone, but the lessons that have come are priceless, and I count them as blessings. I'm trying to allow them to strengthen me and not define me. Because I know if the situation were reversed, you wouldn't. You're the strongest person I know, Gilles. You have always been an example to me and I'm trying to be as strong. I will forever be a work in progress. I know this. I'm so grateful to be able to start each new day with a clean canvas to paint my life on. And when you wake up, you can continue helping me paint it, for us and our baby."

I loved sharing my thoughts him, and I knew somehow he could hear me. Brushing my fingers against his cheek, I kissed him, whispering in his ear, "I have a confession to make. I haven't started reading your notebook yet. I don't know why. Just afraid I guess. But I promise I'll start soon, okay?" I kissed his ear. "I promise."

J. Adams

Chapter 30

The next day, Grace came for another home visit. In fact, she now came there to do all my check-ups. She talked to Gilles for a few minutes and kissed his cheek, saying, "You need to wake up soon, young man, because we have a lot to talk about and catch up on, okay?" I smiled. They would *definitely* have much to talk about.

Dad and Grace had slowly fallen in love. They saw each other every day, even if it was only for a few minutes. They spent as much time together as they could, and when he wasn't working and she didn't have appointments, she was at our home, so it was easy for her to do the check-ups there.

I loved watching Dad and Grace together. Dad had always been an affectionate person. Gina hadn't. I knew he still had his moments dealing with the past, the hurt and loss, but it was great to see him able to express his feelings and affections to Grace and see them genuinely returned.

The night before, Dad proposed to Grace and presented her with a ring. She accepted, knowing that the love between them was unconditional, because he accepted all of her, including her past. I could see the healing power of that love shining from within her. I was excited for their marriage and couldn't imagine a better person for Dad. They planned to marry on New Year's, a little over three weeks away. We all hoped and prayed Gilles would awaken before then so he could be a part of it.

After discussing things with Dad—and completely surprising him with her choice—Grace decided to sell her home, stop taking patients and be a full-time housewife. She said she had put in enough years as a midwife, and now that she was starting a new life with him, she would retire and not look back. However, she did promise to deliver all my babies, so I would have her all to myself. That thought made me smile.

* * *

After Grace left, I folded laundry and put it away, including some of the blankets and sleepers I'd bought for the baby. Thanks to Dad and Grace's help, the nursery was all done. I had ordered the furniture from Salt Lake and it was delivered the week before. Dad put the crib and rocker together and Grace took care of putting up the decor. She gave me her Anne Geddes artwork and hung the framed prints on the nursery walls. Thanks to Tanya and Seth (the two had been an item for weeks and were showing no signs of slowing down) the room was painted two weeks before. Tanya also had a baby shower planned for February.

I was truly grateful for each of them and

considered their presence in my life a blessing.

Even Seth.

Taking the bottle of lotion from the table next to Gilles' bed, I rubbed some on his hands and applied a little Carmex to his lips to keep both from drying out. I closed the shutters just a bit to give him a little shade. When Dad came home, he would help me with other needs. Having taken care of everything, I pulled Gilles' notebook from the nightstand drawer, curled up in the leather chair beside his bed, and opened the book, surprised by what was written there. I took a deep breath and read, tears misting my eyes at the sight of his familiar handwriting.

This is my journal of Giselle,

the most important person in my life.

March, 2006

I went to Seattle last year with Mom and Dad. They went to comfort Adesina, a friend who had just lost her husband. While Adesina talked with Mom and Dad, she asked me to go out to the backyard to check

excited to see me. We went out back and I pushed her on the swing, listening as she told me about her day and the friend she'd made.

Tonight after Giselle changed into her pajamas, we sat and watched a movie. Before it ended she fell asleep with her head on my shoulder. I carried her up to her room and tucked her in. When I kissed her forehead, she gave me that sleepy smile that always melts my heart.

March

It has been two weeks since Giselle came to stay with us and she is slowly adjusting. I only had to sit with her one night this week. Soon she won't need me to and I'll be glad for her, but I will kind of miss it.

She is the most affectionate girl I have ever seen. It doesn't matter how sweaty or dirty I am when I get home, I always get a big hug. If Mom jumps on my case for something, Giselle pops into my room with a sympathetic smile, a warm hug and a kiss on the cheek. Every time she does this, a line from a song by the rock group, Bad English, comes to mind.

> When I see you smile, I can face the world,
>
> you know I can do anything.

That's exactly how I feel. Her loving acts erase any gloom and replace it with sunshine. If I could bottle the happiness she brings, I would be the richest teenager in the world.

Chapter 31

Looking up from the book, I wiped my face and gazed up at Gilles' profile. I had no idea he felt that way about me then. I knew he cared about me, but I never realized how much. Getting inside his head this way was the greatest blessing I could ever ask for, apart from having him awake.

"I love you so much, Gilles. Thank you for sharing your thoughts and letting me read your mind."

July 2006

Today was the best birthday I've ever had and I

know from here on out, they will all be amazing. I turned sixteen and Giselle turned eleven. Mom and Dad took us out for a birthday dinner. Mom wasn't happy about Giselle and me sharing a party. She seemed to think that because I'm five years older, our friends shouldn't occupy the same space, like I needed a big boy party while Giselle needed a kiddie one. But we had a small party anyway and it was great. I got a new car and Giselle got a laptop.

Mom's attitude toward Giselle is something I've never understood. I hope it changes one day.

After the party, my friends wanted me to hang out with them for a while. I didn't really want to go, I just wanted to stay home with Giselle, but I went anyway. There was me, Rick and Dean. We met up with a few girls from the party and hung out at Rick's place for a while.

I got home later than I wanted to. I knew Giselle had gone to bed, but I had an extra present for her that I didn't get the chance to give her. It was a charm bracelet I knew she wanted. She had ripped an ad from one of those fashion magazines and I ordered it a few weeks ago.

I woke her up, but she didn't mind. I apologized about not getting back before she went to bed and she joked with me about being on a date. She had no idea much I wanted to be home instead. I gave her the gift, which she totally loved. I could tell she was surprised and I'm glad I could surprise her.

I've decided that I will surprise my pretty girl with an extra birthday gift from now on.

July

Giselle and I argued today and I never felt so bad in my life. I was supposed to take her and Tanya to a Disney movie after dinner, but I got caught up with Rick and Dean, helping them pick out shirts for a double date they were going on. They had wanted to set me up with a girl from school, but I told them I was busy. Truthfully, I will never go out with the girl. Tracy Glass is one of the loosest girls I know and I could never be into someone like her.

I totally lost track of the time and by the time I got home, the movie had started. Giselle said she couldn't believe I forgot. I got defensive and said I have a life and it didn't revolve around her and her friend. She said I was being mean. I was, and I didn't know why. She went to her room and slammed the door. I couldn't understand why I said what I did and I felt terrible for treating her that way. I still do.

I knocked on her door and asked if I could come in. She said no, so I apologized through the door. I told her how sorry I was and promised I would never let her down again. After a minute, she opened the door. Her swollen, red eyes broke my heart. I knelt down and opened my arms and she ran into them. My height had just hit six-foot-three and she was still so petite, it was like I was holding a little doll. I kissed her cheeks several times and said I was sorry again. She accepted my apology.

Even as I sit here writing this, I am crying because I hurt her so much. But it will never happen again.

I smile, running my fingers across the dried water spots on the page. Gilles' tears.

On and on the entries went, some of them short, some lengthy, but all of them were full introspection of his days, months and years with me. Seeing myself through his eyes made me see him in a way I never have before, and if my love for him could possibly grow anymore, it did with each entry I read.

May 2008

I got in a fight today.

Rick, Dean and Gary, another wrestler on the team, had just showered and were getting dressed when they started talking about what a hottie Giselle had become. Rick said if she were a few years older, he'd go after her and the others laughed. I told them to lay off. They just laughed and kept going. Gary started going too far when he talked about her body and how great she would look in a bikini. Something inside me shifted. Rick and Dean must have seen it in my eyes because they stopped laughing and shut up. But Gary kept going. Then he totally crossed the line when he said something so vulgar and lewd about Giselle that I snapped and hit him in the mouth, busting his lip. He rushed at me, catching me in the stomach, but I barely felt it, I was so mad. I grabbed him and flung him against the lockers. I would have hit him again, but he threw him hands up and said he was done.

He never said another word about Giselle.

I again looked up at Gilles. "Now I know why the knuckles of your right hand were swollen that day."

June 2008

I graduated today. The ceremony was great and it felt awesome to finally be done with school and receive my diploma. Mom and Dad let me have a party and it seemed like half the school was there. Everything was catered, so there was tons of food.

An hour into the party, I caught Rick and Dean staring at Giselle and whispering. Both of them were smiling. When I walked toward her, they looked at my face and I could have sworn they both paled. I told Giselle to go upstairs. The hurt that entered her eyes when I said I didn't want her there almost undid me, but I didn't want her down there being the object of their disgusting thoughts.

I ended the party early and went up, anxious to see Giselle and let her know I didn't mean to make her feel bad. I felt bad enough for both of us. I could hear music and I opened the door. She was dancing, lost in the music. She was so good, so beautiful.

We sat and talked. I apologized for telling her to leave and tried to explain why I did. She understood and was more aware than I realized. I was glad she was. But she is just turning thirteen. She shouldn't have to worry about stuff like that.

After making sure things were okay with us, I kissed her goodnight so we could both get some sleep. We are going to Disneyland tomorrow.

June

Today was our first day at Disneyland and

what a blast we had! Giselle and I hit the rides as soon as we got there. After an hour, Mom said she was tired and wanted to go back to the hotel. Reluctantly, Dad went with her, leaving us by ourselves to enjoy the park. Some family vacation.

I have been to Disneyland before, but being there with Giselle was so much fun. She was fascinated by everything she saw today. The lines for the rides were long, but we didn't mind. We talked and watched people to pass the time. Some of the guys openly stared at Giselle and some would just casually glance. I kept her hand possessively in mine and stared back until they stopped looking. She has no idea how beautiful she is.

The Indiana Jones ride was the last one we went on today. Giselle screamed a couple of times and I laughed, putting an arm around her. She burrowed against me until it was over. When we got off the ride, she said, "I wasn't scared," then smiled that sweet smile of hers, making me laugh. How I adore her! I can't wait to go back tomorrow.

Chapter 32

After going down to the kitchen for a cup of hot chocolate, I returned to my place by Gilles' side and read a little more.

July 2010

This was a very emotional birthday. I had a surprise planned for Giselle. We've always spent our birthdays together, but this time she had agreed to go to a party with Tanya.

Talk about crushed! She promised her friend she would go and I kept thinking, You can't do this!

But I didn't say that. She is fifteen now. It was only a matter of time before things changed and she outgrew our birthdays together. The problem is, things have also changed for me. Inside me.

Somewhere along the line, I have fallen hopelessly in love with Giselle.

Yes, she's only fifteen, but she has had my heart twisting in the wind from the moment we met. I think my feelings for her truly began to change the night of the graduation. I couldn't stand the thought of Rick and Dean or any other guy at the party looking at her. In my head it was brotherly protection. Since then, I have come to realize it was something else entirely.

When Giselle exited the house to go to the party, my heart literally stopped for a moment. She looked so gorgeous she took my breath away. Judging by her expression, she seemed just as unhappy as I was. She asked me to wait up for her and I said I would. I would always wait for her.

She wasn't gone long before she called and asked me to come and get her. When I got there, she cried and apologized. I wrapped her in my arms and said I understood. I was just happy to be able to finish our birthday. I gave her the traditional extra present. It was a locket with a picture of us inside. I then drove her down to Salt Lake for the surprise.

The complete joy on her face as the Royal Ballet Swan Lake played on the screen was priceless. While she watched the ballet, I mostly watch her, taking in her every expression. When it was over, I whispered that I would love to see her dance the part of Odette one day. The look in her eyes as they met mine was one I've never seen before. I reminded myself that she is only fifteen and it probably didn't mean anything. I still remind myself of that.

But I will wait for her. I've always waited for her.

August

Tonight I went out on a date, my first since

graduation. I have tried to avoid it ever since my feelings for Giselle began to change. The few dates I went on during my senior year ended badly for me because as soon as I would kiss them at the door, Giselle's face would pop into my head and suddenly it was her I was kissing. Pushing the image away had not been easy.

Dean set me up with Stefanie Hayes and the only reason I went out with her was to stop all the nagging and keep questions at bay, including Mom's. I've known Stefanie for years and she is a nice girl. She's pretty too, and any guy would be fortunate to be with her. I took her to dinner and a movie. I chose going to a movie mainly because I wouldn't have to converse much. I know it was terrible of me, but I knew nothing would come of going out with her. It couldn't because my heart was already taken.

When I took her home, I could tell she was expecting a goodnight kiss, so I gave her one. But just like before, I imagined I was kissing Giselle and I knew my head was messed up. I felt lecherous thinking about being with her that way, but at the same time it was like I was cheating on her, which was ridiculous really. I've decided I won't be going on any more dates.

Not until I can go with Giselle.

I finally glanced at the clock, surprised at the time. I had spent the whole day reading and now it was time to cook dinner. Dad would be home soon and I wanted to have it ready on time.

Closing the notebook, I stood and stretched. Before heading to the kitchen, I kissed Gilles on the lips. "Reading your thoughts has been amazing, Gilles. Thank you. I love you so much."

* * *

That evening the home health nurse came and took Gilles' vitals, checked his oxygen levels and drew a blood sample. Even though there was no sign of cancer, he was still tested routinely. While she changed the IV bag, I emptied the urine bag. She checked Gilles for bedsores and commended us on taking care of him so well.

After she left, Dad and I bathed him and dressed him in fresh pajamas. I thanked Dad for his help and he left to pick up Grace. They were doing their final Christmas shopping and picking out wedding bands.

My faith that Gilles would wake up was still intact, but it saddened me that he may miss the wedding. Things would be so different when he finally did come back to us.

"Well, one thing's for sure." I said to Gilles as I got ready for bed that night, "You will definitely be rested when you do awaken."

Sometimes I wondered if the whole coma thing was his body's way of resting up and regenerating from all the sickness and treatments, especially since the cancer was gone and they couldn't detect a reason for the coma. When I shared my thoughts with Dr. Peterson during his weekly visit, he said you never know. A deeply religious man, he said there are some things even science can't explain and only God knows. He then said something I found very profound.

"Giselle, the day that the world of science begins to work with God instead of fighting against Him or His existence is the day we will truly discover something special. That will be the day men of science truly begin to understand the mind and will of God, and become open and more like Him. And just think of how far that could take us."

I would never forget that.

I read Gilles' notebook for a while, then forced myself to close it and get some sleep. Kissing him goodnight, I whispered that I loved him and went to bed.

J. Adams

Chapter 33

The following day was spent reading.

December 2012

No words can describe the sight of Giselle onstage dancing the part of Odette in Swan Lake. It was her school's Christmas production and I had been looking forward to it for months. Her performance was flawless and the applause was thunderous. There was a moment when she performed an arabesque and the look on her face left me speechless. For reasons I can't begin to explain, I imagined her dancing for me alone, and that I inspired that look. I quickly took a picture of that perfect moment.

We finally made it backstage to see her and my eyes automatically roamed over her. She was so beautiful. I gave her roses and held her close as she hugged me for a long moment. I could barely let her go, she felt so good in my arms. She is seventeen and becoming all woman, and it showed.

We went out to dinner, and since we always sat next to each other, I kept her hand in mine under the table, just needing to touch her.

When we got home, I wanted to stay up and talk to her, but I figured she was tired and I said goodnight. I was really surprised to hear her soft knock on my door.

I had been writing about her when she came in and quickly put my notebook in the nightstand drawer. I definitely did not want to have to explain that. She sat on the bed and asked me if I really enjoyed the ballet. I couldn't believe she had to ask. I told her I loved watching her and she was amazing. I couldn't take my eyes off her.

She asked me if I got some good photos and I said I did. We talked about the annoying guy who played the prince. It killed me every time he touched her because he seemed to enjoy it too much. She laughed when I told her what I'd like to do to him, then basically complimented me on my body. Seeing her eyes roam over me was almost too much and I felt heat rush through me. Man, what she could do to me with just a look!

When I saw her eyes become teary, I was worried, but she said she was fine, just tired. Tears don't come from being tired. I knew it was something else. We talked about Romeo and Juliet being a lot alike. I told her I could understand the love–boy could I understand the love–but not the destructive choice, because suicide didn't guarantee they would be together but would separate them more. I don't know what I would do in a world where Giselle didn't exist. I wouldn't have to take my life because it would most likely be the death of me anyway.

Giselle said her next ballet would have a

happier ending and I told her it didn't matter what ballet she did. I just loved watching her dance. Then she said, "I like it when you watch me." I just stared at her, unable to speak, the warmth of her words caught me so off guard. She finally leaned in to give me her usual goodnight kiss, but at that moment a kiss on the cheek wasn't enough. So I turned my face a little and her lips landed on the corner of my mouth. Ah, that was heaven! All I could think about was what her kiss would really taste like, how her lips would feel against mine. We finally said goodnight and she left.

And now I will go to bed and spend the rest of the night dreaming about her.

How well I remembered that night. He had no idea how much every moment of it meant to me.

Christmas

It's been an amazing day! And I am so in love!

I pulled Giselle out of bed right on time and we rushed down to hall to wake up Mom and Dad like two toddlers. It has always been that way with us. I was so excited about my gift for Giselle. I love giving her gifts no matter what time of the year it is and I know she prefers things that come from the heart. I hoped she would really like what I got her.

We opened Mom and Dad gifts to us first, then they opened their gifts from us. My turn came to open Giselle's gifts to me. She gave me a scarf that she made herself, a new blue shirt (she always loves blue on me and I like wearing it for the same reason) a scrapbook filled with pictures of us, and a very nice Fossil watch. She whispered for me to turn it over and read the inscription. It said, To G., who is always there. Forever, G.

I finally looked into her eyes, trying to tell her with my gaze how much the inscription meant. Those few words said everything. I thanked her and put it on, struggling to blink the tears away, hoping no one could see just how emotional I was. I smiled and told her to open her gift, anxious for her to see what was inside. I noticed Mom instantly turning her attention to us, which kind of made me nervous for some reason. It wasn't so much that she was watching, just the expression on her face. Totally weird. I could almost believe she suspected something, but she couldn't know.

Giselle unwrapped the small decorative trunk. Everything inside had to do with ballet. I had the words Dream Box engraved on the gold plate attached to the lid at the same time I had the trunk painted. All the things inside were ordered months ago, with the exception of one, and that one thing got the reaction I was hoping for and then some.

I watched the tears fill her eyes and fall down her cheeks as she gazed at the framed 11x13 inch photo I had taken of her as Odette performing an arabesque. I finally felt her eyes on me, but I couldn't look at her or our parents. Still, I was sure she knew what I was hiding. Her voice was soft when she thanked me, but I heard the emotion she was feeling and I had to swallow back my own again.

Then Mom spoiled the moment by commenting on how much money I must have spent on everything. I lied and said it wasn't that much, but truthfully, I really had spent a small fortune. When it comes to Giselle, money doesn't matter. I have my trust and the money I've earned from investments and can do whatever I want with it, plus I make a steady paycheck. If Giselle wanted the moon, I would do my damnedest to give it to her. But she never asks for anything, she always gives, which is why I love her so much.

Later, I found Giselle in her room looking through her gifts again. She looked up when I walked in and her eyes spoke nothing but love. I sat on the floor next to her and we talked for a bit and fell quiet. My heart was pounding as I took her hand, laced my fingers through hers and pulled her closer. When she rested her head on my shoulder, I let my lips travel over her forehead, wanting to kiss her so bad my mouth ached. She only said two words, "Oh, Gilles," and she didn't need to say anything else because I understood.

Sighing, I closed the book. It was so amazing to read in his words the very thoughts and emotions I felt myself that day. It had only been a year since then, but it seemed so long ago. Sometimes it felt like we'd lived a lifetime in the short span of a year.

I stood beside Gilles and brushed my fingers

over his smooth scalp. The hiss of the oxygen was the only sound cutting through the silence. Leaning in and pressing my lips to his ear, I repeated the words I spoke to him each day.

"I need you, Gilles, and so does our baby. I know you hear me and understand. I love you and I know you will come back to us soon. And I will be here, Gilles. I will always be here. You waited for me. Now I will wait for you."

Chapter 34

Christmas came and went. It had been a more subdued one, but it was also spiritual and reflective for Dad and me. We were melancholy but grateful. The year had been filled with highs and lows, but the real meaning of Christmas rang true to us on so many levels.

Grace had suggested that we make a video to show to Gilles when he finally awakened, and we got footage of everything, from treat-making to reading the Nativity story by the tree on Christmas Eve. We videoed while opening presents on Christmas morning

(I was saving Gilles' presents for him) and kept the camera going throughout the day. Doing this helped to make the holiday memorable for us as well.

On New Year's Eve, I tried to convince Dad and Grace to go out and have some fun, but they wouldn't hear of me being home alone, so they stayed in and we rang in the New Year together.

Since all of Grace's things were moved in, she stayed in the main floor guestroom that night. We were all excited for the wedding and went to bed right after midnight.

When I woke up an hour later to use the bathroom, I noticed a light coming from down the hall. I went to Dad's room. The door was open and he was looking at a selection of shirts. He was trying to decide which one to wear for the wedding.

"You would look handsome in a dingy suit and overalls, Dad," I said walking in, surprising him. "Your son sure does."

He turned to me and smiled, but it didn't reach his eyes.

"What's wrong?"

Heaving a deep sigh, he sat down on the bed and I sat beside him. He leaned forward a moment, resting his head in his hand and I rubbed his back.

"Tell me, Dad."

"Giselle, I never expected this to happen. I wasn't even looking for it. I can't think of anything but Grace. Yet part of me feels guilty because it hasn't been that long since . . ."

"I know. But when it's really love, time is irrelevant. And I can see how much you and Grace love each other. You have both been through a lot and you deserve to be happy."

"I do love her. She's an amazing woman."

"She is. And you guys are perfect for each other. Anyone with eyes can see that. If others have a problem with it, then it's their problem."

He smiled and hugged me. "You really do have an old soul. Thank you."

"You're welcome."

"What are you doing up anyway?"

"Bathroom run."

"Oh, yeah. I remember being awake for a few

of those with Gina."

I tried not to let the sudden bout of sadness show as I thought about Gilles not waking with me at night, but Dad noticed.

"I'm sorry, honey," he said, hugging me. "I wasn't thinking."

"Don't be sorry. I'm fine. But I should probably get to bed if I want to get up on time."

"Goodnight." He kissed my cheek. "And thanks again."

"You're welcome."

* * *

Dad's friend, Bishop Nelson–the same man who officiated over Gina's graveside service–performed the wedding. Fittingly, they married on the deck, the same spot where Gilles and I secretly married. Neither of them wanted a big wedding and chose not to invite any other guests.

Grace's dress was a colorful floral sheath that flattered her curves and looked lovely against her brown skin. She topped it with a white cashmere sweater. Dad was dressed in black slacks, a blue shirt and tie, and a dark gray tweed jacket. He was so handsome.

I turned the video camera on and they got started. I was teary as Dad and Grace spoke their vows, and I couldn't help remembering my own wedding day and how happy we were.

Rings were exchanged and they were pronounced husband and wife. They kissed, glowing in their love for each other and I was so happy for them. I now had a mother again and so did Gilles. Because I knew how much he loved Grace, I had no doubt he would be pleased.

"How are you doing, Giselle?" Bishop Nelson asked me afterward. We were sitting at the kitchen table enjoying wedding teacakes and lemon water. The older man had aged a bit since the summer, but kindness still radiated from him.

"I'm fine."

He gave me a sympathetic smile. "How are you really doing?"

There was so much compassion in his voice, I swallowed hard against the rising emotion his words drew to the surface and sighed. "Just taking it one day at a time, taking care of Gilles and holding fast to my faith that he will come through this and everything will be okay." Dad squeezed my shoulder in comfort. I smiled up at him, and then at Grace, sitting across from me. "That's all any of us can do really," I said.

Bishop Nelson was quiet, his eyes fixed on me, his gaze intent. "I would like to do something for you and your husband if that is okay."

"All right."

"I would like to bless your husband. Would that be all right?"

"That sounds fine." I didn't know what that involved, but I was touched by his kindness, and I would never say no to a blessing of any kind. Every prayer helped.

We all went up to my room. For a minute the man stood at the foot of Gilles' bed and simply looked at him. I watched him, puzzled when tears began to trail down his face. After another moment, he moved to the head of the bed, and placing his hands on Gilles' head, he closed his eyes and spoke.

When he was done, we all had tears streaming down our faces. He spoke many things, but one thing stood out to me. He'd promised that Gilles would awaken and be blessed with a long and healthy life . . . but he would awaken at the time God had set and not until then.

We thanked Bishop Nelson and walked him back down. At the door, he asked if he could have a moment with me. Dad and Grace left us alone.

"Giselle," he said, taking my hand, "The Lord loves you and is aware of your joys and sorrows, and he brought you and Gilles together for a reason. He celebrates the love you two share and is proud of you both for your choices and your faith. He is giving you a gift. Accept it, be grateful and make the most of it." Smiling once more, he gave my hand another squeeze and left.

* * *

Two weeks later, Dad received a phone call. Bishop Andrew Nelson had passed away from a year-long battle with brain cancer. He had used his final days to serve others, suffering in silence. And we had no idea.

He was an amazing man.

Chapter 35

I filled the passing weeks and months taking care of Gilles, preparing for the baby, and reading Gilles' *Book of Giselle*.

June 2013

I kissed Giselle tonight for the first time. As I held her in my arms, pressed her body against mine and tasted her mouth, my mind couldn't form a single coherent thought. It was everything I dreamed it would be and more.

June

Yesterday Giselle and I married in secret,

pledging before God to love each other forever. It was the most spiritual experience of my life. And making love to her last night was an extension of that experience. Becoming one with her was amazing, incredible, and celestial. I've never known such a feeling. Owning Giselle's love and having her own mine is a rare and precious gift.

July

Today I found out I am going to be a dad.

Today I also lost my mother in two ways–when she turned her back on Giselle and me, and when a car accident took her life. It was a day of death and new life, and joy and sadness are at war within me.

For now, the sadness has earned its day.

There were two pieces of paper between the pages. I unfolded them. One was the Romeo letter I wrote to him in Verona. The other was a poem from one of his favorite books.

The Human Potential

The day we can look within ourselves and see our mortality,
yet feel the worth of our souls,

*the day we can look on others and see the goodness in
them
despite their weaknesses,*

*the day we can say no to evil,
despite the evildoings of those around us,*

*when we can cry with those who suffer,
mourn with those who bear loss,
and comfort those who cast your comfort aside,*

*when we can see the good in each new day
and recognize the gifts that come with that day,*

*when we can love with a pure heart,
expecting nothing in return,
and magnify our valiance to the fullest,*

*the day we set aside the cares of the world
and embrace every good thing with a singleness
of mind, heart, body, and soul,*

ever faithful, ever vigilant, doing all within
our power to remain unchanged in all respects,

on that day, we become more than mere men—
we become gods
and we live forever.

I slipped it back between the pages. The fact that this was one of Gilles' favorite pieces said so much about him and the kind of man he was.

* * *

Two days before our little one was due, I finished reading the last entry, seeing yet another side of Gilles, uncovering another layer of his goodness, his compassion, and his unconditional love.

Today I have been pondering some things I have learned from loving Giselle.

First: Whenever I am trying to be my best self, my best is good enough. Because she is so easy to love, I always want to be my best self and be worthy of her.

Second: When you really love someone, sacrificing something for that person is no sacrifice, it is a privilege, no matter how great the thing is you're giving up.

Third: Just like plants need water, forgiveness is essential for growth. An unforgiving heart is a stunted one. Giselle is the most forgiving person I know.

Last week as Giselle and I placed flowers on Mom's grave and took a few moments to silently ponder her life, it came to me just how short this life is, putting so many things into perspective. One day we will come to see and understand how significant we all are. We will see that all the little things we place value on, all the grudges and hates we hold on to, are all so small. The former should be put in its proper place the latter should be let go. The things that last beyond this life are the ones that are the most valuable.

Fourth: Love is definitely a verb. And there is nothing I love more, or that makes me happier, than loving Giselle.

Fifth: Human kindness is what makes us human.

I've also learned that it's possible to be so connected to someone that the two of you become one mind. When that happens, it is impossible to hurt them without hurting yourself.

One of my favorite quotes is from Immanuel Kant. "Rules for Happiness: Something to do, Someone to love, Something to hope for." I have all these and more, so I must be the happiest man on the planet. Man is placed on this earth that he might have joy. Giselle is my joy, and the child she carries in her womb is a product of that joy. We are taught that we should be thankful in all things. I've been blessed with all I could ever want.

How could I not be thankful?

Closing the notebook, I clutched it to my chest and cried. The entry had been written three days before he went into the hospital. He was feeling terrible, yet he could still pen such gracious thoughts.

Moaning, I slowly rocked back and forth, longing for the warmth of Gilles' arms. It had been so long since I felt them around me, and I missed being wrapped up in him with an intensity that made my whole being ache.

My labor was beginning. The contractions I had been having since the day before were starting to increase in intensity and frequency. Glancing at the portable tub Grace had set up near Gilles' bed, my tears also increased. I had thought he would be helping me with the birth that he would be kneeling beside the tub, helping to support me while I gave birth to our baby. We planned and dreamed and talked about how his would be the second face our child saw. Accepting that this wouldn't be was a struggle now, and I began to pray for comfort and for the strength to do it without him.

Gazing over at my husband, I *was* quickly comforted. That comfort came with the knowledge that he was home with me, alive and cancer free. That's what was important.

Needing to touch him, I went to him and caressed his head, gently running my fingers over the dark stubble now covering his scalp. His brows and lashes were also starting to grow back and a small bit of gruff shadowed his face. Breathing deeply, I waited for another contraction to pass.

"Our baby is coming soon, Gilles. If it's a girl, she will be beautiful, and if it's a boy, he will look just like you, totally gorgeous." I took one of his hands in mine. "He will be tall and strong like you when he's older, and you can teach him to wrestle. I will teach our daughter to dance. Before long she will be Odette." I kissed his hand, my breath catching as another contraction came.

Grace came in. "How are you doing?"

"They're stronger."

"How far apart?"

"Five minutes."

"All right." She uncoiled the hose and started filling the pool, taking a minute to adjust the temperature until it was right. While it filled, she bustled around the room, setting up the birthing equipment and supplies. She brought in a space heater and turned it on. "Okay, why don't you go and change and relax while I get everything ready. I'll call your dad with an update in a bit."

I went into the bathroom and changed into a

short, sleeveless sleep shirt. Standing in front of the mirror a moment, I examined my reflection, my heart full of mixed emotions. Gilles never got a chance to see me fully pregnant. He missed out on rubbing essential oils on my stomach, back and feet like he'd looked forward to. He missed out on trying to distinguish the baby's body parts as it poked and stretched inside me. He missed out on all the things that came with the anticipation of seeing your child for the first time after waiting so long, and finally holding that child in your arms. Would he feel cheated when he finally awakened?

Stop it, Giselle. I shook off the dismal thoughts. A few minutes later, my water broke. I grabbed some towels and quickly cleaned the floor. As soon as the tub was filled, I got in. My contractions were about two minutes apart by then and the water was soothing, calming the pain almost immediately. I looked up at Gilles where he lay, grateful we could be together for this, even though he couldn't see it. Having him there would be enough.

Grace put a relaxation CD in the player and

turned the volume on low, and within an hour I was pushing, a burst of energy filling me. Two minutes later, our little boy entered the world, his transition peaceful. The moment was an ethereal, spiritual experience and tears immediately filled my eyes as I held him against me. He was beautiful, absolutely beautiful and perfect.

"Oh, Gilles," I said softly as I gazed at our son, "I wish you could have seen it. I wish you could see him." I smiled, kissing the baby's soft cheek.

"I see him, babe," came Gilles' hoarse voice. Grace and I both gasped and looked up. His head was turned toward us and he was smiling, a tear sliding across the bridge of his nose. "I saw everything."

Epilogue

Gilles

Sitting on the deck with his arms around his wife and son, Gilles smiled as his father snapped their family photo. It was Antonio's first birthday and they had just celebrated with a small party. They were still dressed in their church clothes, wanting to look nice for the picture. Gilles sighed, holding his little family close, and for the millionth time thanked God for giving him a second life.

Waking up to Giselle giving birth to their son should have been a shock to his system and completely jarring, but it hadn't been. He had marveled as he watched the miracle unfold, Giselle and Grace completely unaware that he was conscious. Emotionally, he was exhausted afterward and had fallen asleep quickly. When next he awoke, Dr. Peterson was there, examining him, shaking his head, calling it a miracle and declaring he'd never seen anything like it in his life. Other than weakened muscles and weight loss, there was absolutely nothing wrong. Gilles had listened to the doctor's comment about Giselle's thoughts on his body needing a recuperative rest and had asked her about it at another time, fascinated by her insight. She also told him about Bishop Nelson and Gilles was filled with humility and gratitude for the man's sacrifice.

Rehabilitation had been slow but steady, and before long, Gilles was active and robust again, regaining his weight and muscle tone, thanks to a bit of exercise, a healthy appetite and good genes. Giselle and his dad and new mom filled him in on all he'd missed, and he watched the holiday and wedding videos several times. He could never get those four months back, but every detail he was given helped him to feel like he had been there.

Once Gilles was well enough, he never missed an opportunity to make love to his wife, and like a depleted soul quenching an undying thirst, she absorbed all he gave, making up for all the time they were deprived of each other's touch.

He spent three days a week at his shop. The rest were spent with Giselle and the baby. During the three hours a week that she taught dance, he took care of Antonio, rocking him, talking and singing to him. His son did look like him, only slightly tanner.

After they finished taking pictures and Antonio was taking a nap, Gilles and Giselle went to their room and she gave him a gift as well when she drew his head down and whispered in his ear, "I'm pregnant."

Sitting on the bed, he pulled her onto his lap and kissed her, rich warmth moving through him as the taste of her mouth and the sound of her soft moan reached inside him, drawing from him an answering groan. Lying back on the bed and rolling her beneath him, he kissed her again, then parted his lips from hers and whispered with a grin, "I guess making up for lost time is paying off."

She chuckled. "I guess it is. But I don't mind, do you?"

He smiled, tears blurring his vision of her face for a moment. "Never."

* * *

William Blake said, "Love seeketh not itself to please, nor for itself hath any care, but for another gives its ease, and builds a heaven in hell's despair." When Gilles lay in a coma, there were times when I had truly felt hell's despair, and because of the love we shared, faith built me a small heaven, soothing my anguish.

But as I lay wrapped in Gilles' arms, I understood then. The small heaven I experienced before was only a taste of what awaited me, for now I was experiencing paradise. And though I couldn't imagine it getting any better, I knew it would, and with the passing of time things would shift and grow. And with that growth would come the opening of our eyes.

God did put us here that we might have joy.

And oh, the joy!

About the Author

J. Adams has written books in different genres, but her main focus is inspirational interracial romance. She is a motivational speaker to both youth and adult audiences. In her spare time (when she has any) you can find her curled up with a good book and a healthy stash of orange Tic Tacs.

She and her family reside in Utah.

Email: jewela40@gmail.com
Websites:

gisellesrain.weebly.com

JewelAdams.com

The Rainy Season

www.ingramcontent.com/pod-product-compliance
Lightning Source LLC
Chambersburg PA
CBHW071257170626
46809CB00001B/250